The Weight of Silence

Adelaide Vaughn

Published by Adelaide Vaughn, 2024.

This is a work of fiction. Similarities to real people, places, or events are entirely coincidental.

THE WEIGHT OF SILENCE

First edition. October 7, 2024.

Copyright © 2024 Adelaide Vaughn.

ISBN: 979-8227056016

Written by Adelaide Vaughn.

Chapter 1: The Echo of Silence

The air in the studio feels electric, charged with an undercurrent I can't quite place. The familiar neon glow of the "On Air" sign casts an almost surreal light over my workspace, transforming the mundane equipment into something significant. The dull buzz of the city outside is a constant reminder of life moving on, of stories unfolding that I'm not part of, while I sit here, cocooned in the dim glow of my own little world. I press my lips together, tasting the familiar tang of the coffee I spilled earlier—an unintentional casualty of my jitters. It sits cold and forgotten next to me, a silent testament to my growing unease.

"Alright, you've got this!" Ellie's voice slices through my reverie, warm and encouraging. She leans against the soundboard, a sly smile dancing across her face. "Just remember, you're not a robot. It's okay to feel."

I roll my eyes, a practiced motion that comes too easily. "Right, because emotions are what everyone tunes in for." I can't help but grin. She's right, of course, but the last thing I need is to be vulnerable on the airwaves. Vulnerability invites chaos, and I have enough of that in my life. I've meticulously built these walls, stone by stone, and they are not coming down for a voice, no matter how gravelly or intriguing.

But as I cue up the next song, that voice lingers, a ghost in the back of my mind. It's not just what he said; it's how he said it. There was something raw, something genuine, tucked behind the gruffness. And I can't shake the feeling that he, like me, was searching for something—a connection, maybe, or simply a release from the loneliness that cloaks so many of us like a second skin.

The next hour flies by in a blur of music and muted chatter, but my thoughts drift back to the call. It's not like I've never had strange callers before. Some are heartfelt, some just downright odd. But this one—this one felt different, like I had unwittingly opened a door I didn't know existed.

"Hey, Miss Mysterious," Ellie chimes in, snapping me back to reality. "You've been awfully quiet tonight. Is that a sign of a budding romance I sense?" Her teasing tone is light, but I can see the glimmer of genuine curiosity in her eyes.

"Please," I scoff, waving her off as I lean into the microphone, adjusting my posture. "You know I don't do romance." The words come out sharper than I intended, but it's the truth. I've built my life around avoiding entanglements, sticking to my solitude like a protective shield. "It's just a voice, Ellie. A distraction."

"Yeah, but it's your distraction," she counters, her eyebrows arching. "And a pretty compelling one, at that. Who knows, maybe he's your soulmate, calling from the depths of radio hell."

I chuckle, shaking my head as I cue another track. "Right, my soulmate is sitting in a dark room somewhere, clutching a phone, waiting to pour his heart out to a late-night radio host. How romantic." I try to suppress the flush creeping into my cheeks, but the image lingers—what if he really is out there, longing for someone to reach out to him, just like I am?

As the minutes slip by, I can't help but steal glances at the clock. Time feels fluid tonight, slipping through my fingers like sand. I wait for the moment when I can end my shift, but something pulls me back, tethering me to this space. Just as I'm about to push through the final hour with my usual playlist, the phone rings again, a shrill sound that cuts through my thoughts.

Ellie raises an eyebrow, surprised, but I'm already reaching for the receiver, my heart racing.

"Good evening, you're on the air," I say, my voice steady, but it's a lie. Inside, I'm a bundle of nerves, a tight coil ready to spring.

"This is him," the gravelly voice rumbles, and my breath catches. It's like hearing an old song I thought I had forgotten—familiar, comforting, and deeply unsettling all at once.

"What do you want?" I ask, half-joking, half-expecting him to back off. But the way he laughs, low and warm, sends a shiver down my spine.

"I wanted to hear your voice again," he says, each word dripping with an intimacy I didn't know I craved. "You sounded... different tonight. Like you actually cared."

I blink, stunned. My thoughts race, swirling into a mess of confusion. Was he really picking up on something, or was this just a figment of my overactive imagination?

"Don't flatter yourself," I retort, trying to regain control of the conversation. "I don't have time for games. This isn't a dating service."

"Maybe not," he replies smoothly, "but don't you think the airwaves could use a little romance? A bit of chaos? After all, isn't that what makes life interesting?"

The challenge hangs between us, palpable, daring me to step outside the confines I've carefully constructed. I can't deny the truth in his words. Life is chaotic, a beautiful mess of unexpected moments, and yet here I am, stuck in my perfectly curated silence.

"Who are you?" I ask, curiosity mingling with a hint of defiance. "You just call in and throw a grenade into my routine? What's your game here?"

There's a pause on the line, heavy with thought, and for a fleeting second, I imagine him sitting in a dimly lit room, perhaps the same as mine, with an air of mischief dancing on the edges of his voice.

"Maybe I'm just someone looking for an escape. Just like you."

The words hit me harder than I expected, a revelation swirling in the dim light of the studio. An unexpected twist in a life otherwise governed by predictability.

"Then welcome to the club," I respond, a flicker of laughter in my tone, unsure if I want to encourage him or slam down the phone. But something in me aches to keep the conversation going, to explore the hidden depths of this stranger on the other end of the line.

It's almost laughable how quickly the night shifts with the echo of that call still ringing in my ears. The studio, usually my fortress, now feels more like a stage where I'm perpetually performing, the audience on the other end not just passive listeners but participants in this dance of dialogue.

"What if he's just some creep?" Ellie's voice breaks through my spiraling thoughts, her eyebrow arched, arms crossed. "I mean, you don't know him. You could be inviting trouble."

I let out a dry chuckle, but her words hang in the air like a stubborn smoke. "Trouble is my middle name, remember? Or maybe it's 'Disaster.'" I lean back in my chair, putting on a brave face. "But seriously, I've dealt with worse." The bravado feels flimsy, even to me. The truth is, my shield against the world has been heavily reinforced over the years, and letting even a tiny crack show is terrifying.

The clock ticks loudly as I prepare for the next segment. I scan the playlist—some safe classics to smooth over the jagged edges of my evening. Yet, as I cue the next track, the rhythmic pulse of the music isn't enough to drown out the anticipation swirling in my chest. It's been years since I let someone's voice linger like this, and the realization is unsettling. I quickly switch gears, filling the silence with light chatter about the weather and local events, my tongue dancing to a well-practiced routine.

Just as I'm finding my groove again, the phone rings, the shrill tone piercing through the soft music. My pulse quickens at the familiar sound, my hand reaching for the receiver almost instinctively.

"Welcome back to the echo of silence," I say, half-expecting to hear his gravelly voice again.

Instead, I'm met with a giggle, light and airy, a sharp contrast to the gravity of my previous caller. "Hi! Is this the late-night therapy hotline?"

"Only if you're paying in existential dread and half-empty coffee cups," I quip back, trying to shake off the tension.

THE WEIGHT OF SILENCE 5

"Well, I've got a whole truckload of that!" she replies, her laughter warm enough to melt the ice forming around my heart.

I find myself smiling, a genuine smile this time, even though I can't see her. "What's your name?" I ask, curious.

"Call me Iris," she says, her voice like sunshine peeking through clouds. "I just wanted to call and share my unsolicited life advice. I heard your last segment about being alone in a crowded world, and I had some thoughts!"

"Hit me with it, Iris," I say, intrigued despite myself.

"Okay, picture this: You're on a deserted island, right? Only you and your thoughts. And then—bam! A ship shows up!"

"A rescue ship?" I interject, feeling a burst of warmth as the absurdity of her imagery wraps around me like a soft blanket.

"Nope! Just a bunch of weirdos wanting to start a beach volleyball tournament."

I burst into laughter, the sound freeing, dispelling the tension that's gathered like storm clouds in the corners of my mind. "Well, at least they're trying to have fun! I'd probably just throw coconuts at them and demand to be left alone."

"That's exactly what you shouldn't do! You've got to embrace the chaos, my friend!" she insists, her tone playful yet insistent. "You might just find a new reason to enjoy the isolation. Maybe some of those weirdos would become your friends."

"Friends?" The word feels strange on my tongue. I've gone so long without really letting anyone in that it sounds foreign, like a note from a forgotten song. "I think I'd rather stick to my coffee and the occasional heartfelt call."

"Pfft! Coffee doesn't cuddle! You need to break out of your shell!" she declares, and I can almost see her shaking her fist, rallying against my defenses.

Iris's spirited banter carries me through the next few minutes, and for the first time in ages, I feel something shift within me. Maybe it's the fact that she's a stranger, her opinions uncolored by my past; perhaps it's the possibility of new connections that my heart yearns for.

As I steer the conversation back toward lighter topics—favorite movies, music, the strange way avocado toast has taken over brunch menus—an unexpected vibration reverberates in my pocket. My heart drops as I pull out my phone, the screen flashing with a name that sends a chill down my spine. It's not Iris; it's the last person I expected to hear from.

"What's wrong?" Iris asks, her voice suddenly serious, keenly aware of my shift in demeanor.

"Just... a blast from the past," I mumble, trying to hide my surprise.

"Do I need to unleash my inner therapist?" she quips, though her tone is laced with genuine concern.

"Not unless you're good at dealing with family drama," I reply, swallowing the bitterness that comes with the thought.

"Bring it on!" she declares, and before I know it, I'm pouring out snippets of my life that I've tightly sealed away. The complicated dynamics of my family, the relentless pressure to fit into their mold, and the realization that I've been running from them for so long that it's become second nature.

"Wow, that sounds exhausting," Iris sympathizes, her tone softening. "But let me tell you this: you're not just running from them; you're running toward something better. That's what matters."

I feel my heart swell at her words. A stranger, yet she understands me better than I've allowed anyone to in years. But before I can respond, the ringing stops abruptly, and I'm left staring at my phone, the last lingering words of my family fading into the background noise of my studio.

"Are you okay?" Iris asks, sensing the abrupt end to my thoughts.

"I think I am," I reply, my voice quiet as the world outside my studio becomes a distant hum. "I think I really am."

But just as the moment feels safe and cozy, like wrapping myself in my favorite blanket, the studio door swings open with a loud creak. Ellie bursts in, her face a canvas of excitement mixed with urgency.

"I'm sorry to interrupt, but you won't believe who just walked in," she breathes, eyes wide, a mix of delight and mischief. "It's—"

Before she can finish, the lights flicker, a sudden power surge plunging us into darkness. The music cuts out, leaving an eerie silence where the connection to the world outside feels tenuous. My pulse races as I grasp the phone tightly, the only lifeline in this surreal moment.

"Ellie, what's happening?" I call out, my voice breaking the stillness.

Iris's voice crackles through the phone, a soft beacon in the dark. "Hello? Are you there?"

But before I can respond, I hear footsteps—heavy, deliberate, approaching the studio. My breath catches in my throat, fear curling around my heart.

The door creaks again, and I feel an ominous presence behind it, leaving me suspended between fear and curiosity, just like the moments before a storm. I glance at Ellie, who's frozen in place, her eyes wide with anticipation.

"Who is it?" I whisper, a knot forming in my stomach as I grip the phone tighter.

The figure looms, shadowy and indistinct, and just as I'm about to call out, the door swings open, revealing a face I never thought I'd see again, with a smirk that sends chills down my spine.

"Surprise," he says, and suddenly, everything I've built—my carefully constructed isolation, my controlled life—feels like it's on the brink of unraveling.

Chapter 2: Waves of the Past

The next morning, I regret how easily I was rattled. Sitting across from Ellie in our favorite coffee shop, I'm acutely aware of the rich aroma curling around us like a warm embrace, contrasting sharply with the crisp chill of fall in Boston. The leaves outside flutter like small, anxious birds, their golden hues dancing under the weak sunlight filtering through the café window. Ellie, with her tousled auburn hair and contagious laughter, pulls me back into our conversation. Her latest escapade involves a date gone sideways, complete with an ill-timed magic trick that left her date more embarrassed than enchanted.

"Honestly," she says, rolling her eyes as she takes a sip of her latte, "who thought pulling a rabbit out of a hat could be a relationship dealbreaker? I thought we were beyond that."

I chuckle, my lips curving into a smile, but my thoughts drift like a kite caught in a breeze, soaring towards last night. The voice, deep and resonant, reverberates in my mind, its familiarity a riddle I can't solve. A chill settles in my stomach as I attempt to brush it off, blaming my restless mind and the haunting chill of autumn. Perhaps I should have paid more attention to Ellie's story instead of letting that voice seep into the cracks of my psyche.

Later, I decide to take a stroll through the old part of the city, a patchwork of history and nostalgia woven into the brick buildings lining the streets. I pass the quaint little shops that sell artisanal chocolates and handcrafted wares, their windows displaying treasures that beckon the eye. Each step I take on the uneven cobblestones brings forth a symphony of memories I've worked hard to bury.

Suddenly, I'm swept away to a sunlit afternoon spent in this very city, the vibrant laughter of friends echoing around me. But alongside those bright memories is the weight of a darker past—a part of me I thought I'd locked away in a dusty attic of my mind. Ethan. The name rolls off my tongue like a bittersweet song. My ex, my best friend, the only man I ever let close enough to hurt me.

We were inseparable, Ethan and I, until the love that tied us together became a noose, strangling the laughter out of our bond. I remember the way he looked at me, his gaze a mix of admiration and something deeper—an understanding that terrified me. We danced in the kitchen of our tiny apartment, flour dusting our noses, music playing softly in the background as we created culinary disasters. Those moments felt sacred, as if we were crafting our own little universe, untouched by the outside world.

But love is fickle, isn't it? It can transform from sweet honey to bitter ash in an instant. I had watched us crumble under the weight of unspoken words and misunderstood intentions. The pain of loving him too deeply, only to see it all fall apart, still stings like a raw wound.

As I meander through the streets, I find myself wandering towards the studio where I'll be showcasing my art tonight. The air is thick with the scent of impending rain, and the clouds hang low, heavy with unspoken promises. When I reach the entrance, the studio seems almost alive, the walls whispering secrets of artists who have come before me. I step inside, the familiar sounds of bustling preparation wrapping around me like a worn blanket. The chatter of fellow artists, the clinking of glasses being set for tonight's gathering—it all feels comforting and chaotic at once.

But tonight, everything feels different. My thoughts are jumbled, a tempest brewing within as I arrange my pieces for display. The colors of my paintings reflect my emotional turmoil—fiery reds clashing with cool blues, swirling together like the chaos in my heart.

As I lose myself in the rhythm of preparation, the voice calls again, echoing through my mind like a dark melody. My heart skips a beat. This time, he lingers on the line a little longer. "I see you, the girl behind the mic," he says, his tone oddly intimate, as if he's peering into the depths of my soul.

I feel exposed, stripped bare before a stranger who somehow knows me better than I know myself. It sends a thrill of both fear and excitement coursing through me. What does he want? What could he possibly know about me? I tuck a loose strand of hair behind my ear, trying to steady my breath as I fight the urge to respond. But the phone goes silent, leaving me stranded in my own confusion.

"Hey, are you okay?" Ellie's voice pulls me from my thoughts, her brow furrowed in concern. I hadn't realized she had walked in.

"Yeah, just... lost in thought," I say, forcing a smile that feels more like a mask than genuine joy.

"Is it about the show?" she asks, her eyes glinting with curiosity.

I nod, but the truth lingers on my tongue, a half-formed confession I'm not ready to voice. The voice from the night before feels like a shadow creeping into my light, and I don't want to burden her with my doubts.

"It's just the usual pre-show nerves," I add, trying to sound casual.

She raises an eyebrow, the skepticism evident in her expression. "You're going to crush it. You always do. Just remember why you started doing this in the first place."

Her encouragement washes over me, a balm to my frayed nerves. But as I step back into the world, preparing for the night ahead, I can't shake the feeling that something, or someone, is waiting for me just around the corner, ready to pull me deeper into a past I thought I'd left behind. The night hums with potential, a melody of excitement and dread, and I'm not sure whether I should dance along or brace myself for the storm.

The hustle and bustle of the gallery filled the air as I set up for the show, a cacophony of laughter and chatter that twirled around me like confetti. The dim lighting cast a soft glow over my paintings, illuminating their vibrant colors, but my mind remained shrouded in a haze. Each stroke of the brush had been a catharsis, yet as I prepared to share this piece of my soul with the world, anxiety knotted in my stomach.

"Do you want me to hang these or just throw them on the floor?" Ellie called from the other side of the room, where she was juggling the last few canvases like a circus performer.

"Please don't throw them!" I shouted back, forcing a grin to mask my swirling thoughts. "I might need to sell them for therapy."

She rolled her eyes but smiled, her laughter bubbling like champagne. "Honestly, who needs therapy when you have a friend who's essentially a walking, talking emotional train wreck?"

The gallery door swung open, letting in a draft that sent a shiver up my spine. I glanced over, expecting to see a few familiar faces trickling in, but instead, I was met with a tall figure clad in a dark coat that hugged him like a shadow. He stepped into the light, revealing striking features that seemed all too familiar. My breath caught in my throat, and I nearly dropped a paintbrush.

"Ethan," I whispered, barely audible over the lively din. The name felt heavy, laden with memories that swirled like a tempest in my heart.

He stood there, uncertain and yet undeniably magnetic. I could feel the air around us change, thickening with the weight of unspoken words. It had been years since I'd seen him, and yet the memory of his laughter and the way he used to look at me, like I was the only person in the room, flooded back in a dizzying rush.

"What are you doing here?" I managed to ask, my voice a mix of surprise and a tinge of something else I couldn't quite place—hope, maybe?

"I heard about the show and thought I'd come see your work," he replied, his voice deep and steady. It was a stark contrast to my racing heart. "You always had a way of capturing things that others couldn't."

"Thanks," I said, trying to maintain composure as I leaned against the nearest easel, suddenly feeling like I was on a tightrope without a safety net. "That's... kind of you."

He stepped closer, his eyes sweeping across the canvases, a flicker of admiration lighting them up. "Your talent is incredible. I knew you'd make it big one day."

The compliment sat between us, hanging like an unsaid apology. I wanted to ask why he hadn't been in touch, why he had vanished without a trace, but the questions felt too heavy. Instead, I glanced back at the paintings, searching for solace in the colors that told stories I wasn't sure I was ready to share.

Just then, the voice echoed in my mind again, slicing through the moment like a hot knife through butter. "I see you."

I flinched, a wave of unease washing over me. "Do you ever feel like your past is, I don't know, just lurking around the corner?" I asked, half-joking, but the tremor in my voice gave me away.

Ethan raised an eyebrow, his expression softening. "Like an ex who doesn't know when to let go?"

I laughed, though it was more of a nervous chuckle. "Exactly that. It's like I'm haunted by the ghosts of my choices."

"Let's not get too existential here," he teased, his smile returning, the warmth of it melting the chill in the air. "This is supposed to be a celebration, right?"

"Right," I echoed, my heart still racing, but with a spark of hope now weaving through the trepidation. "Let's toast to that."

He lifted an imaginary glass, and I couldn't help but mirror the gesture. "To celebrating our shared emotional trauma!"

"Cheers to that!" I laughed, the sound of it feeling a little more genuine.

As the evening unfolded, guests arrived in waves, their laughter mingling with the clinking of glasses and the soft notes of a local band playing in the corner. My initial nervousness began to ebb as I engaged with friends and patrons, each compliment about my work wrapping around me like a cozy scarf.

But Ethan lingered on the periphery, his presence a warm glow that both comforted and unsettled me. I caught glimpses of him, exchanging words with other artists, yet his gaze would often find me, igniting something I thought I'd buried deep.

As the night progressed, a subtle tension settled in the air, something electric that hummed beneath the surface of our friendly banter. Just as I was about to approach him, the voice invaded my thoughts once more, echoing like a distant memory. "I know who you are."

I gripped the edge of my canvas, the moment stretched taut like a drawn bowstring. The lights seemed to flicker, the noise of the gallery fading into a dull hum, leaving only the pounding of my heart. My mind raced, each thought colliding with the next. Why did it feel like I was on the precipice of something monumental?

Suddenly, a shrill laugh broke through the fog of my confusion, and I turned to see a woman with sharp features and a confident stance approaching Ethan. She had an air of effortless glamour, her smile bright but calculated, like a tiger in a garden.

"Ethan, darling! I didn't expect to see you here," she said, her voice smooth as silk, dripping with an undertone I couldn't quite decipher.

My stomach twisted.

"Hey, Claire," Ethan replied, his tone friendly but distant, like a lighthouse on a foggy night.

I tried to sidestep the growing knot of jealousy tightening in my chest. Who was she? A flash of possessiveness surged through me, and for a moment, I struggled to breathe. It felt like a weight pressing down, leaving me grappling for air amidst the laughter and chatter.

"Are you two old friends?" Claire continued, a sly smile playing on her lips as she looked between us, as if weighing the dynamic in the air.

"We used to be," I interjected, my voice sharper than I intended.

Ethan shifted slightly, caught off guard. "Yeah, we were close once."

The air between us grew thicker, a taut string pulled to its limit. I could almost hear the unspoken tension crackling around us. Claire's gaze narrowed, and a hint of amusement danced in her eyes, like she was privy to a secret she wasn't ready to share.

"Interesting," she said, the word hanging heavy with implication.

As the night wore on, I felt as if I were trapped in a twisted game where the rules were made up on the fly. I was acutely aware of every glance, every sidelong smile shared between Ethan and Claire, the way their chemistry crackled in the air.

"Let's get a drink, shall we?" Ethan suggested, pulling me gently toward the bar, his voice low and conspiratorial.

"Yeah, let's," I replied, my heart racing as we moved away from Claire, the relief washing over me like a cool breeze.

But as I turned to face him, I caught the glint of something in his eyes—a spark that felt all too familiar and yet utterly foreign. "What's going on with her?" I asked, trying to keep my tone light, though my heart pounded as if trying to escape.

He hesitated, the weight of the question hanging in the air. "Claire is... complicated."

Before I could probe further, the lights flickered again, and the gallery door swung open, slamming against the wall. A figure stood silhouetted in the doorway, their breath visible in the chilly air. The crowd fell silent, and a shiver crept down my spine as I recognized the unmistakable outline.

"Did I miss the party?" the voice called out, sending a jolt through me that felt like lightning. It wasn't just any voice. It was the same voice that had echoed through my mind earlier, the voice that had sent chills cascading down my spine.

My heart raced, and the room began to spin as I processed the weight of those words. What did he want? What did he know? And why did it feel like the past was crashing back to reclaim me? The atmosphere thickened, a storm brewing just beyond the horizon of my understanding, and I couldn't help but brace myself for the tempest ahead.

Chapter 3: Unraveling Secrets

I'm restless. Something about that voice is eating away at me. The cadence lingers in my mind like the aftertaste of dark chocolate—bitter yet sweet, utterly tantalizing. I turn the dial of my radio show, flipping through segments that barely hold my attention. Ellie's voice, bright and lively, dances around me like a wisp of smoke, but it feels distant. It's the magnetic pull of the mystery caller that keeps my thoughts tangled in an echo of his words. I can't shake the way he leaves me hanging, every pause laced with anticipation, like a cliffhanger in a book I'm dying to finish.

With a sigh, I pull myself from the chair, the faux leather squeaking in protest. My feet lead me toward the door, as if some unseen force has mapped out a journey for me. I find myself driving through familiar streets, but each bend in the road feels alien now, coated in a thin film of nostalgia and regret. The old bookstore on the corner appears like a mirage in the distance, its sign swinging lazily in the warm breeze, the paint peeling, yet charming. I park the car and step out, the smell of rain-soaked pavement and the faint scent of fresh ink enveloping me.

Inside, the air is thick with the aroma of old paper and coffee, a comforting embrace that wraps around me like a warm blanket. Dust motes float in the sunbeams filtering through the windows, dancing to a tune only they can hear. I stroll down the narrow aisles, fingertips grazing the spines of well-worn novels, each one a portal to a different world. I can't help but smile, recalling the afternoons spent here with Ethan, our laughter echoing off the walls as we debated characters and plots, our conversations blurring the lines between fiction and reality.

I reach for a book with a tattered cover, a volume we once cherished. A bittersweet smile tugs at my lips. My heart aches for the boy who used to sit across from me, his eyes sparkling with mischief and wisdom. I left a part of myself in this place, and now it feels like an echo, a haunting reminder of what once was. The bell above the door chimes as another customer enters, jolting me back to the present. I force myself to look away from the past, and I'm struck by the brightness of the café tucked into the far corner, where the barista—a whirlwind of energy with colorful hair—whips up lattes and pastries with the precision of a magician.

"Do you have the usual?" the barista asks, her eyes sparkling. I can't help but laugh; it's as if she knows me better than I know myself.

"Actually, I think I'll try something new today," I reply, surprising myself. It feels like a tiny rebellion against the monotony that has clung to me lately. I order a caramel macchiato, extra foam, and take a seat by the window, where the sunlight spills in like honey, warming my skin.

I cradle the cup in my hands, feeling the heat seep through the ceramic. The clatter of cups and soft chatter creates a comforting backdrop, and for a moment, I lose myself in the rhythm of life around me. Yet, the nagging feeling returns, that itch beneath my skin that compels me to pick up my phone and check for missed calls or messages. The number isn't saved, a faceless caller whose voice dances on the edge of my consciousness. He's elusive yet compelling, like a half-remembered dream I can't shake off.

As if on cue, my phone buzzes against the table. I glance down, my heart racing as I see that familiar number flash on the screen. It's him. I take a deep breath, the world around me fading into a blur as I hit the accept button.

"Hello?" My voice is steadier than I feel, laced with curiosity and a hint of something else—excitement, maybe.

"Do you remember the first time we met?" His voice rolls over me, smooth and rich like the coffee I'm sipping.

I don't have to think long to recall that day. It was a chance encounter at a bookstore much like this one, but in a different city. I had been hunting for a rare edition of my favorite novel when he'd nudged me playfully, offering me a suggestion that turned into hours of conversation.

"Of course I do," I reply, a grin spreading across my face. "You told me I'd regret not reading the last page first. I thought you were mad."

His laughter dances through the phone, a sound I could get lost in. "And yet, here we are, both still reading between the lines."

"Why do you keep calling?" I ask, my voice steadying, a hint of challenge beneath my words. "You can't keep weaving these vague threads of conversation without revealing something substantial. It's infuriating and thrilling all at once."

"Is that what it is for you?" he muses, his tone contemplative. "Infuriating? I thought we were enjoying the mystery."

"Enjoying is a stretch," I retort, crossing my arms defensively, though the warmth creeping into my cheeks betrays my true feelings. "It's maddening. You're like a puzzle with half the pieces missing."

"And yet, you keep coming back to it," he replies smoothly, the satisfaction in his voice evident. "Maybe there's something about the unknown that draws you in."

"Or maybe it's just you," I shoot back, feeling emboldened. The banter is like a dance, fluid and spontaneous, a rhythm I didn't know I needed.

"Touché," he concedes, a hint of admiration in his voice. "But don't you want to know more about me?"

"Of course," I say, the words spilling out before I can rein them in. "But you have to give me something more than riddles and smoke. I don't need another mystery to solve."

He pauses, and the silence stretches between us like a taut string, ready to snap. "How about this? I'll tell you my secret, but you have to promise to share one of yours in return."

I lean back in my chair, weighing the proposition. There's something deliciously reckless about it, as if I'm standing at the edge of a cliff, teetering on the brink of something exhilarating. "Fine. You first."

"Fine. You first." The challenge hangs in the air between us, electric and palpable, like a live wire begging for a spark. I can practically feel the anticipation vibrating through the phone, igniting every nerve ending in my body.

"Alright," he begins, his voice dropping to a conspiratorial whisper that sends shivers down my spine. "I'm not really who you think I am."

"What do you mean?" I lean forward, my heart thumping in sync with his words. "Are you an undercover agent? A secret superhero? A misunderstood villain from a novel?"

He chuckles, the sound rich and layered like the coffee swirling in my cup. "Not quite. I'm just a guy who likes to hide behind the curtain. My real name isn't even what you think it is. I have a habit of reinventing myself, and I've gotten a bit carried away."

"Okay, I'm intrigued. So, what is your real name? Or is that part of the mystery?"

"It's Lucas," he says, the name flowing like a melody through the receiver. "But you can call me whatever you want. I think the way we connect is far more interesting than any label."

"Lucas," I repeat, letting the name roll off my tongue. It feels familiar, yet foreign, like a favorite song that's been covered by someone new. "So, what's the deal with the mystery? Why all the theatrics?"

He pauses, a thoughtful silence stretching between us. "It's simple, really. I've been through a lot, and sometimes it's easier to hide than to face the truth. But with you, it feels different. I want to share, but I'm terrified."

"Terrified? Of me?" I can't help but smirk. "Come on. I'm a hot mess, and you're the one who's pulling my heartstrings from the other side of the line."

He laughs, and the sound is light yet laden with something deeper. "That's exactly why. You're a whirlwind, and I'm afraid of getting swept away."

My breath catches at the unexpected admission, and for a moment, I feel raw and exposed, as if I've peeled back a layer of my own protective armor. "You know, you could always choose to take a risk. Sometimes the best things come from stepping out of our comfort zones."

"Is that what you're doing now?" he counters, a teasing lilt in his voice. "You're so eager to know me, yet you keep dancing around the truth about yourself."

"Touché," I reply, feeling the heat of his gaze even through the phone. "Fine. I'll play your little game. My turn. Here's my secret: I've sworn off relationships. I don't do heartbreak anymore."

"Is that so?" His tone shifts, curiosity piqued. "Is that why you're stuck in this cycle of unease? Running from something or running to someone?"

"Maybe both," I admit, the weight of my own words sinking in. "After Ethan, I didn't think I could bear the pain of losing someone again. It felt safer to build walls than to risk getting hurt."

The silence that follows is thick, the kind that begs for a gentle nudge. "And yet, here you are, talking to a stranger," he finally replies, voice softening. "Doesn't that mean something?"

"It means I'm curious," I counter, feigning nonchalance even as my heart races. "Or maybe I'm just really good at making bad decisions."

"Or maybe you're finally allowing yourself to feel again," he suggests, his voice low and soothing. "Sometimes the best things are just outside our comfort zones."

His words wrap around me like a warm embrace, igniting a flicker of hope deep within my chest. Maybe he's right. Maybe it's time to confront my fears instead of running from them. But just as I'm about to dive deeper into the conversation, a loud crash echoes in the café, sending my heart leaping into my throat.

I turn instinctively toward the source of the sound, my eyes widening as I spot a stack of books tumbling off a nearby shelf, cascading to the floor in a chaotic heap. The barista darts across the room to assess the damage, her vibrant hair swaying with her every hurried step.

"Sorry!" a voice calls from the back, a sheepish-looking man emerging from the aisles, his hands raised in surrender. "I didn't mean to cause a scene!"

"Nice save, Romeo," I mutter under my breath, chuckling at the unexpected twist of the day. "It seems I'm not the only one making bad decisions."

"Are you okay?" Lucas asks, his voice laced with concern.

"I'm fine. Just a little distracted, that's all." I force a laugh, but my mind is racing, trying to make sense of the unexpected interruption. "Let's focus on the secrets, shall we?"

"Sure, but I'll need to hear another secret from you first," he teases, his tone lightening the mood.

"Fine," I huff, rolling my eyes playfully. "I'm afraid of commitment. There, I said it. Happy?"

"I think you're afraid of losing yourself," he counters, his voice steady, a tone that feels like a solid ground beneath my swirling emotions. "But you have to understand that love doesn't mean losing yourself. It means growing together."

"Easy for you to say, Mr. Mysterious," I retort, feeling the air crackle between us. "You've got it all figured out."

"Hardly," he replies, the sincerity in his voice disarming me. "I'm just a guy trying to figure it all out, too. If I'm honest, I've been running from something myself."

"What is it?" I lean in, eager to unearth whatever buried truth he's hiding.

"Something that could change everything," he admits quietly, the weight of his words sinking deep into my chest. "If I let you in, it might shatter the illusion I've created. And I can't risk that."

"Then maybe we both need to take a leap," I suggest, my heart racing at the vulnerability in his tone. "Let's drop the facade, Lucas. I'm ready if you are."

"Ready or not, here comes the truth," he breathes out, and I can almost picture him on the other side of the line, his brow furrowed in thought. "But first, I need to know if you really want to know me or if you're just playing a game."

"I'm done playing games," I reply, the conviction in my voice surprising even me. "If you're ready to reveal the real you, I'm all in."

But just as his response hangs on the tip of my tongue, the line goes dead, and my heart plummets, a stone dropped into an abyss. I grip the phone tightly, staring at the screen as if it holds the answer to this sudden silence.

"Lucas?" I whisper, my voice barely audible over the café's din.

Nothing. Just an empty void where his voice used to be. The world around me continues to bustle, the barista laughing with a customer, but my heart beats wildly in my chest, pounding out a frantic rhythm of uncertainty.

Then, as if answering my unspoken fears, my phone buzzes again, this time with a text. I swipe it open, breath hitching as I read the words that flash on the screen:

I'm sorry. I need to go. It's not safe.

The world tilts on its axis, a sense of impending chaos creeping in, and for the first time, I truly feel the weight of the secrets we've been dancing around. I glance around the café, suddenly hyper-aware of every detail—the way the sunlight catches the dust motes, the distant sound of laughter, and the unmistakable feeling that I've only scratched the surface of a much deeper mystery.

Chapter 4: Collision Course

The night air was thick with the hum of city life, a soft cacophony of distant sirens and the occasional honk of a cab cutting through the silence. I shuffled toward my car, fatigue weighing heavily on my shoulders, my mind still buzzing from the live show that had just wrapped. The studio had been electric, as it always was, but this time there was an undercurrent, a thread of tension that ran deeper than the usual mix of excitement and nerves. It was as if I had cracked open a puzzle box only to find more pieces than I could ever fit together.

I paused as I neared my car, spotting the crumpled note flapping against my windshield. A flicker of anxiety prickled at my skin, like static electricity before a storm. My breath caught in my throat as I leaned in closer, my heart pounding in sync with the rhythm of the city's pulse. The note was written in hasty, uneven script, the kind that screamed urgency and secrecy. It was just a line from a song I had played during the show, one that had stirred memories I wasn't quite ready to confront.

"Let the river run..." it read.

The familiar melody swirled in my mind, a bittersweet tune that held echoes of summer nights and laughter shared beneath a canopy of stars. But the sentiment felt twisted now, tinged with something darker. My pulse quickened, the shadows of the empty street pressing in around me. Who had left this? A fan? A prankster? Or was it something more sinister?

I turned, scanning the street for any sign of movement. The dim streetlights cast long shadows, and for a moment, I imagined a figure lurking just beyond the periphery of my vision. I shook my head, chiding myself for letting my imagination run wild. But the tight knot in my stomach wouldn't loosen, the sensation of being watched prickling along my spine.

As I slid into the driver's seat, I glanced at my phone. No messages, no missed calls—just the flickering light of my screen reminding me that life outside this moment was blissfully mundane. But what if it wasn't? What if this caller, the one who had begun to infiltrate my thoughts like an unwanted guest, was connected to this cryptic note? I couldn't shake the feeling that there was a thread weaving through all of this—a connection just waiting to be unraveled.

Ellie's voice echoed in my head, her well-meaning warnings about getting too caught up in my work. "You're not a detective," she had said, rolling her eyes at my growing obsession. But she didn't understand the pull this mystery had on me. It was like a dark, swirling vortex, and I was helplessly drawn in. Every call, every detail shared made my mind race, igniting a fire of curiosity that I couldn't extinguish. The thrill of the chase was intoxicating, even as it spiraled me closer to the edge of something unknown.

I gripped the steering wheel tightly, forcing myself to breathe. I needed to separate work from life, to anchor myself back in reality. But as I turned the key in the ignition, the engine roared to life, a comforting sound in the otherwise eerie stillness. I decided to drive, to let the city's heartbeat drown out the noise in my head, to pull me back to a place of clarity.

The streets were quiet, the nighttime glow of neon signs flickering like stars that had fallen from the sky. I drove aimlessly, letting the city guide me through familiar neighborhoods that held memories—late-night coffee runs, laughter spilling from open car windows, and the electric thrill of unexpected encounters. But tonight, every corner turned felt laden with weight, every shadow seemed to whisper secrets I couldn't quite grasp.

Pulling into a small diner that had become my refuge, I stepped inside, the bell above the door jingling in greeting. The comforting scent of bacon and burnt coffee enveloped me like a warm embrace. It was just the kind of grounding I needed. I slid onto a barstool, leaning forward to order my usual—coffee, black, strong enough to burn the edges of my sanity into submission.

"Rough night?" the waitress asked, a knowing smile tugging at her lips as she poured my drink. She had seen me enough to know the signs.

"Just the usual chaos," I replied, forcing a smile, but my thoughts were miles away, still tangled in the web of uncertainty. I glanced around, taking in the late-night patrons—two tired truckers sharing a booth, a couple whispering secrets over milkshakes, and a lone man in the corner, his face shadowed by a newspaper, as if he were hiding from the world.

But it was the waitress's knowing gaze that caught my attention, a flicker of curiosity dancing in her eyes as she placed my coffee in front of me. "You look like you've seen a ghost," she quipped, her tone light but with an undercurrent of concern.

"More like I'm haunted by one," I replied, my voice a mix of humor and desperation. "You ever get that feeling like something's about to change? Like the world's holding its breath just for you?"

She raised an eyebrow, leaning in slightly. "Oh, honey, if you're waiting for the world to breathe again, you might be waiting a long time."

Her words struck a chord, and I couldn't help but laugh, the sound easing some of the tension coiling in my chest. There was wisdom in the simple truth of her statement, a reminder that life was always a series of collisions—moments that could alter our course with no warning.

With my coffee steaming in front of me, I took a sip, letting the bitterness coat my tongue as I wrestled with the chaos brewing inside. I had to make a decision. I could either let this spiral consume me or seize the narrative, regain control before it spiraled into something beyond my reach.

My phone buzzed on the counter, pulling my attention back to reality. I picked it up, my heart racing as I saw the caller ID flash across the screen. It was him—the caller who had become an enigma in my life, a riddle wrapped in a voice that both soothed and unsettled. I hesitated, a mix of dread and excitement coursing through me. Maybe this time, I would get answers.

Taking a deep breath, I answered. "Hello?"

And just like that, the world shifted again, the air crackling with possibility, and I knew this collision course I was on was only just beginning.

The voice on the other end was smooth, almost velvety, wrapping around my thoughts like a cozy blanket on a chilly evening. "Hello?" It wasn't the casual greeting I expected; there was an undertone of urgency, a hint of something that had been waiting to surface. "I've been waiting for your call."

The world around me blurred into insignificance as I tried to comprehend the weight of those words. "Waiting? You knew I was going to pick up?" My tone was a mix of incredulity and cautious curiosity, both emotions vying for dominance.

"Of course," he replied, his voice calm and steady, like a lighthouse beacon piercing through a storm. "You've been doing a lot of thinking lately. It's evident in your questions."

My heart raced at the implication, a mix of excitement and dread coiling within me. "Are you stalking me?" I half-joked, though I could feel a chill creep along my spine at the mere suggestion.

"Not stalking. More like… observing," he said, his laughter dancing on the edge of amusement. "You're like a puzzle I can't quite solve, and I do love a good challenge."

I fought to keep my composure, my grip tightening around the phone. "Is that what you call it? A challenge?"

"Isn't it? Every clue you've uncovered has only deepened the mystery."

"Right," I said, rolling my eyes even though he couldn't see me. "And what's your endgame? What are you hoping to find?"

"Maybe it's not what I'm hoping to find, but what you need to discover about yourself," he replied, his tone shifting slightly, almost earnest. "You're unraveling, and I think you're afraid to admit it."

The audacity of his words struck me, and I felt the sharp prick of anger mixed with embarrassment. "You don't know anything about me."

"Or maybe I know more than you think. You've been grappling with something profound, haven't you? Letting someone else in can be terrifying."

A wave of heat rushed through me, and I clenched my jaw. How dare he? "You don't get to psychoanalyze me, especially not when you're hiding behind a phone call."

"Touché," he said, amusement threading through his voice. "But maybe it's time you step out from behind your own walls. What's stopping you from confronting whatever it is that holds you back?"

His words hung in the air, a challenge wrapped in intrigue, and I felt a flicker of uncertainty in my chest. This wasn't just some random caller; he was wielding insights like weapons, sharp and precise. I didn't want him to know how deeply his words pierced, but a part of me knew they were true. "You're assuming a lot," I countered, trying to reclaim some ground. "I'm fine. I'm just busy."

"Busy dodging your own truths. You can deny it, but that won't change the reality of the situation."

The gravity of his words weighed on me, each syllable like a stepping stone leading me deeper into an abyss. I exhaled slowly, trying to regain my footing. "What do you want from me?"

"I want you to ask better questions, to dig deeper. To truly see what's right in front of you."

The call ended abruptly, leaving a cold silence in its wake. I stared at the phone, bewildered by the conversation. What was that supposed to mean? There was an unsettling quality to the exchange, a sense that

I had crossed into a realm of shadows and secrets, and I was standing right on the precipice.

I took a moment to gather my thoughts, but the familiar diner buzz faded into the background. The waitress came by, her hands carrying a plate of fries that wafted warmth into the air. "You look like you just saw a ghost again," she quipped, eyes sparkling with mischief.

"I'm beginning to think I might be haunted," I replied, picking at the fries absentmindedly.

"Well, if ghosts are all you have to worry about, I'd say you're in pretty good shape." She winked and moved on, leaving me to ponder her words.

As I chewed on the crisp fries, my mind raced with possibilities. Was the caller a ghost of sorts? A specter from my past trying to draw me out of my own haunted existence? The more I thought about it, the more I felt trapped in a web of his making. I couldn't let myself spiral too far down this rabbit hole; I had to keep my wits about me.

Yet, every time the phone buzzed with a notification, my heart leaped into my throat. I couldn't shake the feeling that the mysterious caller would return, but would he come as a friend or a foe?

Hours passed, and as I finally prepared to leave the diner, I noticed something on the table next to mine—a small, weathered book. It was bound in dark leather, its spine cracked with age, the title faded. I picked it up, flipping it open.

It was a collection of poems, the pages filled with elegant scripts and rough sketches. But what caught my eye was the final page, marked with a thin slip of paper. My breath caught as I unfolded it. The handwriting was unmistakably the same as the note left on my car.

"Let the river run. Follow the current, and you'll find what you seek."

I glanced around, the cozy diner now feeling claustrophobic, the shadows stretching and shifting. This couldn't be a coincidence. The pieces were connecting in a way that sent chills dancing down my spine.

I looked at the waitress, but she was busy tending to another table, her back turned to me.

I had to get out of there, to breathe fresh air and shake the creeping sensation that I was being drawn deeper into something far beyond my control. I shoved the book into my bag, my heart racing as I dashed out into the cool night.

The streets were quiet, but I felt the tension in the air, electric and alive, as if something monumental was about to happen. I hurried to my car, but as I approached, the feeling of being watched returned. My instincts screamed at me to run, but I forced myself to look around, every shadow feeling like it harbored a secret.

And then I saw him. A figure leaned against the lamppost at the end of the street, shrouded in darkness. My heart stopped as I met his gaze, a smirk playing on his lips, an all-too-familiar shape emerging from the shadows.

I was caught in a collision course between fear and curiosity, and as he stepped forward, I felt the world tilt on its axis. "I see you found my book," he said, his voice low and smooth, wrapping around me like silk and steel.

And in that moment, I knew my life was about to change forever.

Chapter 5: Shadows in the Rain

Rain drummed against the windshield like a metronome, each drop a reminder of the tension coiling tighter in my chest. I glanced in the rearview mirror, my heart lurching as I caught sight of the same car again. Its headlights glowed in the darkness, a distant but ever-present echo of dread. I gripped the steering wheel, knuckles whitening as I turned onto a side street, my pulse quickening with every tight curve. This wasn't paranoia; it was a reality I could no longer dismiss.

Pulling into my driveway, I inhaled sharply, forcing myself to breathe. I could almost hear Ellie's voice in my head, a gentle nudge to rationalize the situation. "You're just imagining things," she'd say. But reality and imagination had blurred into a tangled mess, and I felt like I was standing in the eye of a storm, with chaos swirling just outside my vision. I needed to talk to someone, someone who could tell me I was overreacting. I fumbled for my phone, but the weight of it felt heavy in my hand, a brick of dread and uncertainty.

Inside the house, the warm glow of the lamps did little to chase away the chill creeping into my bones. I tossed my keys onto the table, the jingle echoing in the stillness, and padded into the kitchen. The comforting scent of coffee still lingered, a reminder of the quiet mornings I cherished. But tonight, it felt more like a stranger than a friend. I made my way to the window, pulling the curtain aside to peer out. The rain fell harder, painting the world in a watercolor blur. No sign of the car. Just the rhythmic patter against the pavement, a reminder that everything outside felt just as lost as I did.

I flicked on the television, hoping to drown out the unease with some mindless entertainment. As the characters bantered on screen, their laughter felt dissonant against the fear that churned in my gut. I sank deeper into the couch, the fabric clinging to my skin like a second layer of dread. My phone buzzed, jolting me from my stupor. It was

Ellie. I hesitated, letting the vibrations fade into silence before finally answering.

"Hey, you," she chirped, her voice a balm against the cold. "You still alive?"

"Barely," I replied, my voice lacking its usual sparkle. "I'm just... you know, working too much."

"Right. That's why you sound like a ghost. What's going on?"

I paused, weighing my options. Do I tell her? The last thing I wanted was to worry her more than necessary. But the need for connection clawed at me. "I just feel... off. Like I'm being watched or something."

There was a silence on the other end, a pregnant pause that felt heavy with unspoken words. "What do you mean, watched? Are you serious?"

I sighed, rubbing my temples. "It's stupid. Probably just my imagination running wild. It's been a long week."

"Not stupid. Tell me more."

I recounted the note and the unsettling sensation of being followed. As I spoke, I could hear the worry creeping into her voice, a low hum that threatened to envelop us both. "Okay, you're freaking me out a bit," she admitted, her tone half-serious. "But seriously, let's meet up. We can do a movie night, eat junk food, and you can distract yourself. How does that sound?"

"Yeah, that sounds great," I said, grateful for her enthusiasm, even as a weight settled in my stomach. I could already hear the muffled laughter and the crackle of popcorn, but would it really be enough to dispel the shadows lurking just outside my window?

"Great! I'll bring the snacks. We'll binge-watch something that'll make us forget life exists. Just no horror movies, okay? I don't need any nightmares tonight," she said, her laughter brightening the darkness around me.

After we hung up, I felt a flicker of hope, but it was short-lived. The sky seemed to grow darker outside, the clouds pregnant with rain. I found myself standing at the window again, a prisoner to my own thoughts. I wished for the clouds to lift, for the storm to pass.

But then, a flash caught my eye—a quick, almost imperceptible movement just beyond the streetlight's glow. I squinted, pressing my forehead against the cool glass, my breath fogging the surface. A figure stood there, a silhouette in the rain. My heart raced, pounding against my ribcage like a caged bird desperate to escape. Just as I was about to turn away, the figure moved closer, merging with the shadows, swallowed by the darkness.

I stumbled back, the coffee mug slipping from my grasp, shattering on the floor like my tenuous grip on reality. The shards gleamed like tiny stars in the dim light, but there was no beauty here, only fear. I forced myself to breathe, to think rationally. Maybe it was just a trick of the light, a fleeting illusion conjured by my overactive imagination.

But that thought barely had time to settle before a sudden knock echoed through the house, sharp and jarring, shattering the fragile peace I had tried to construct. I froze, the sound reverberating like a gunshot in the silence. The world outside was a tapestry of rain and shadow, and I was tangled in its threads, a moth caught in a web of uncertainty.

I braced myself against the door, the sharp rap still ringing in my ears. The world around me narrowed to that sound, a persistent reminder that I wasn't alone, whether I liked it or not. I took a tentative step toward the door, the hardwood creaking beneath my weight as I peered through the peephole. The rain continued its relentless assault outside, streaking down the glass like a curtain shielding me from whatever lay beyond.

"Hey! I know you're in there!" The voice was familiar, dripping with frustration and a hint of humor. It was Ellie, sounding more determined than I'd ever heard her. "Are you hiding from me or just contemplating the meaning of life? Because if it's the latter, you're in for a long night."

Relief washed over me, almost as refreshing as the rain-soaked air. I opened the door just wide enough to let her slip inside, her presence flooding the room with warmth and laughter. "You scared me half to death," I said, trying to muster a smile, but I felt more like a deer caught in headlights.

"Good," she replied with a grin, shaking off her umbrella and letting a cascade of water droplets escape into my hallway. "The world needs a little more panic. Now, where's the popcorn?"

As I turned to head into the kitchen, I couldn't help but feel a flicker of normalcy return. Ellie's buoyant spirit always had a way of lifting my mood, even when shadows threatened to engulf me. I poured us each a glass of wine and set the popcorn to pop, the comforting sounds of kernels bursting echoing through the kitchen.

"Okay, spill," she said, plopping down on the couch with a dramatic flourish. "What's really going on? You were dodging my questions like a pro."

I sighed, curling up next to her, the weight of the past few days settling like an unwelcome blanket on my shoulders. "It's just... this feeling. I can't shake it. Like there's someone out there watching me. And then there was the knock tonight, and I thought—"

"Did you actually see anyone?" she interrupted, her brows knitting together in concern.

I shook my head, avoiding her gaze. "No, but I saw a figure outside before you knocked. I'm probably just being ridiculous."

Ellie took a sip of her wine, contemplating. "Listen, if someone's out there, we're going to figure it out. You're not going to face this alone." She reached over, squeezing my hand. "What if we put your paranoia to work? We can turn it into a movie plot. Just think: 'The Mysterious Stalker Who's Just a Neighbor with a Really Weird Hobby.'"

I chuckled despite myself, the tension in my chest easing ever so slightly. "I could write a bestseller. 'How to Be Completely Unhinged in Five Easy Steps.'"

"Exactly! But for now, we're going to watch something that requires zero brainpower, preferably featuring a handsome lead and a lot of explosions."

With a flick of her wrist, she grabbed the remote and began flipping through the channels until she landed on a mindless action flick. I leaned back, letting the movie wash over me, even as my thoughts flickered like the screen's changing colors.

But as the film progressed, my mind wandered, drifting back to the feeling of being watched, the distant headlights trailing me, and the figure lurking in the rain. I couldn't shake the dread tightening around my heart, threatening to swallow me whole.

A sudden crash of thunder startled me from my reverie, and I jumped, spilling a bit of my wine. "Didn't see that one coming," Ellie said, stifling a laugh as she reached for the napkins.

"Maybe we should change the movie to something less intense. Like... kitten videos?" I offered, my voice trembling slightly.

"Kitten videos? Are you trying to turn me into a cat lady?" she shot back, her eyes gleaming with mischief. "What's wrong with you? We're here to embrace chaos, remember?"

I couldn't help but laugh, the sound breaking through the tension like sunlight breaking through clouds. But just as I began to relax, a flicker outside my window caught my eye. My laughter died in my throat as I turned to look, heart racing.

"What's wrong?" Ellie asked, glancing over her shoulder.

"Nothing... just thought I saw something," I muttered, trying to sound casual. I was stalling, the instinct to protect her kicking in. I didn't want her to worry any more than she already was.

"Just something or someone?" Her voice turned serious, the laughter evaporating like the storm clouds outside.

I swallowed hard, my mind racing. "Just someone," I confessed, barely above a whisper. "I thought I saw a shadow."

Ellie's expression shifted from playful to concerned in an instant. "You know what we should do?" she said, her voice barely above a whisper now. "Let's go check it out."

"Are you insane? We're not going out there!" I blurted, my heart pounding in my chest. The very thought of stepping into the night felt like stepping into a trap.

"Look, I get it. You're scared, and I don't blame you. But if there's something out there, wouldn't you rather face it together? We could do this. We're like the dynamic duo of overthinking!"

I shook my head, torn between wanting to protect her and the urge to face this fear. "I don't think we should. I just... I just want to pretend everything is fine for one night."

"Pretending doesn't fix anything," she replied, standing up and straightening her shirt as if preparing for a battle. "I'm going out there, and you're coming with me. If there's a monster lurking outside, I refuse to let you face it alone."

She took my hand and pulled me toward the door. I hesitated, the shadows outside now feeling more ominous than ever, but the warmth of Ellie's grip anchored me. "Okay," I finally said, my voice barely above a whisper. "But if I get eaten, I'm haunting you."

As we stepped outside, the rain whipped around us, each drop a cold reminder of the night ahead. The street was eerily quiet, the kind of silence that stretched and pulled at the edges of my mind. But Ellie marched ahead, her determination palpable.

Suddenly, a figure darted across the street, cloaked in darkness, the movement so swift it sent a chill racing down my spine. "Did you see that?" I whispered, clenching Ellie's hand tighter.

She nodded, eyes wide with shock. "Yeah, I did. And I don't think it's just a neighbor with a weird hobby."

Before I could respond, a shadowed form stepped out from behind a tree, soaking wet and shrouded in darkness. My breath caught in my throat, fear wrapping around me like a vice as the figure took a step closer, their face obscured.

"Who's there?" I called out, my voice shaking but resolute, a last desperate attempt to assert some control over the situation.

But the figure only laughed, a low, unsettling sound that sent shivers down my spine. "You've been asking questions. It's time for answers."

My heart raced, and in that moment, I knew we were no longer the hunters, but the hunted, standing on the precipice of a revelation that would change everything.

Chapter 6: A Voice Too Familiar

The studio buzzes with its usual energy, a swirl of muted voices and the persistent hum of electronics that fill the air like an electric fog. I lean back in my chair, fingers dancing over the smooth surface of the console, while my heart beats a chaotic rhythm in my chest. Tonight's show had gone surprisingly well, filled with laughter and light banter. But that familiar weight presses down on me like a storm cloud, threatening to burst at any moment. I take a deep breath, but the air feels heavy, laced with something I can't quite identify—fear, anxiety, or perhaps a shadow of hope?

The phone rings again, shattering my fleeting sense of calm. It's a calling card for my late-night program, a lifeline for the lonely souls who tune in when the world outside goes dim. I'm about to dismiss it when a rush of curiosity surges through me. I answer, my voice bright and cheerful, but the moment he speaks, that cheerful facade shatters like glass.

"Do you remember the lake?" he asks, the words laced with a familiarity that sends chills skittering down my spine.

My heart plummets into my stomach, and I grip the receiver tighter, as if that will somehow anchor me to reality. No one knows about the lake. It was our sanctuary, Ethan and mine—a hidden slice of paradise tucked away beneath the towering pines, where the sunlight danced on the water's surface like scattered diamonds. It was a place we went when the weight of the world became too much, a refuge from the chaos that life sometimes threw our way. But that was years ago. How could he possibly know?

"Who is this?" I manage, my voice steadier than I feel.

"Just a friend," he replies, a sly undertone curling through his words. It's infuriatingly cryptic, a riddle I want to solve but can't quite grasp. My pulse quickens, each beat echoing in my ears like a war drum, drowning out the ambient noise of the studio. "I've missed you, you know."

I blink, caught off guard, but the familiarity in his tone makes my skin crawl. "Missed me?" I echo, skepticism heavy in my voice. "You must have the wrong number."

"Oh, I assure you, I have the right one," he insists, the amusement in his voice cutting through the static. "Tell me, do you still go there?"

"What do you want?" I shoot back, my heart racing. I know I shouldn't engage, but a morbid curiosity compels me. "Why are you doing this?"

"Because I wanted you to remember," he says simply.

The line goes dead, leaving me breathless, suspended in disbelief. I hang up, my mind a whirlpool of confusion and dread. Is it really him? After all these years? The memories flood back like a tidal wave—Ethan's laughter, the warmth of the sun on our skin as we lounged by the water, our whispered secrets mixing with the rustle of leaves overhead. How could he have found me? And why this strange game of cat and mouse?

I shake my head as if trying to dislodge the memories. It's impossible. I close my eyes, the studio fading into darkness as I retreat into my thoughts. But the sound of his voice still lingers, a phantom echo of a life I thought I had buried deep within my past.

Morning light seeps into the room, splattering golden rays across my desk, illuminating the hastily scribbled notes from last night's show. But the words blur together, the thrill of my job dulled by the weight of the unknown. I try to focus on the tasks ahead—editing segments, responding to listeners, planning future shows—but the lake looms in my mind like an unwanted guest, unsettling and persistent.

I decide to pay a visit, compelled by a need to confront the past head-on. The drive through the woods is familiar, the winding road lined with towering trees that seem to stretch endlessly towards the sky. Memories flood back—Ethan's laughter, the teasing glances, the shared dreams that had felt so tangible, so real. I grip the steering wheel tighter, knuckles whitening as the anxiety mounts within me.

When I arrive, the sight of the lake stuns me into silence. It's as beautiful as I remember, a perfect mirror reflecting the deep blue of the sky above. I step out of the car, the crisp air biting at my skin, and the sound of the water lapping gently against the shore calls to me. Each step feels heavy, as if the ground itself is reluctant to let me move forward.

"Ethan?" I whisper, my voice swallowed by the trees. The word hangs in the air, a desperate plea mingled with hope.

The wind shifts, carrying the scent of pine and something else—something familiar that sends a shiver down my spine. I turn, half-expecting to see him standing there, with that playful smile and twinkling eyes, but there's nothing but the silence of the forest and the gentle rustle of leaves. I feel the weight of the world pressing down on me again, as though I'm being watched from the shadows.

Just when I think I'm alone in my anguish, a voice calls out from behind me, smooth and teasing. "I thought you'd never come back."

I spin around, my heart racing, and there he stands—Ethan, as strikingly handsome as I remember, with that infuriating smirk plastered on his face, making my heart do a somersault. My breath catches in my throat, a mixture of shock and a thrill I had thought long extinguished. I take a step back, disbelief and a tangle of emotions coiling tightly within me.

"What are you doing here?" I demand, trying to keep my voice steady. "You have some nerve showing up after all this time."

His grin widens, that same playful glint in his eye that once made me feel invincible. "I always knew you'd come back. You can't resist the call of the lake, can you?"

The accusation in his tone tugs at something deep within me, a memory I can't quite place. My heart races, the tension thick between us, thick enough to cut with a knife.

"You have some nerve showing up after all this time." My voice is sharper than I intend, but I can't help it. It's as if every unresolved feeling I've ever had about Ethan collides in a fiery explosion inside me. There he stands, looking like a dream and a nightmare all at once, his casual confidence igniting something both thrilling and terrifying.

"Is that any way to greet an old friend?" he retorts, eyebrows arched in that infuriatingly charming way I remember all too well. "I mean, I thought we had something special."

"Special? You vanished without a word, Ethan! Do you know how many birthday candles I blew out waiting for you to call? How many times I replayed our last conversation in my mind, trying to understand what went wrong?" Each word spills out, a torrent of frustration, and I regret the emotional flood but can't seem to stop. "And now you just pop up here, at our lake, acting like nothing ever happened?"

He steps closer, his expression softening. "I know it looks bad, but I—"

"You have no idea how it looks!" I cut him off, my heart racing as adrenaline fuels my indignation. "You just had to know the one place I'd be vulnerable, didn't you? You had to play this twisted game."

His gaze holds mine, a storm brewing beneath the surface, and I can see the conflict within him. "It's not a game. I wanted to reach out, but... I wasn't ready."

"Not ready for what? To explain yourself? To tell me why you left without so much as a goodbye?" I shake my head, my voice quivering with an intensity that feels almost foreign. "You don't get to just show up and pretend everything's fine."

"I thought about you every day," he says, his voice low, almost raw. "Every. Single. Day."

I look at him, the weight of those words settling in the air between us. "Then why didn't you come back? Why didn't you call?"

A beat passes, a fragile silence enveloping us like a shroud, the sounds of nature echoing our emotional stalemate. The wind rustles through the trees, mimicking the turmoil brewing in my heart. "I was in a dark place. I didn't want to pull you into it," he finally admits, his eyes searching mine for understanding.

"Is that supposed to make me feel better? Knowing that you thought abandoning me was a good idea?" I cross my arms defensively, yet a part of me aches at his admission. The vulnerability in his voice chips away at my anger, and I wonder if, deep down, I still want to believe in him.

"Do you think it was easy for me?" he challenges, his brow furrowing as he steps closer, his presence both grounding and disorienting. "Leaving you was the hardest thing I've ever done. But I thought it was the right choice—for you, for both of us."

"Right choice?" I scoff, anger bubbling back up. "And what's changed? You think you can just waltz back in here, make me relive our memories, and somehow everything will magically be okay?"

Ethan's gaze softens, and the sincerity in his eyes knocks the wind from my sails. "I'm not here to ruin anything, Lexi. I'm here to make things right."

"Right how? By playing mind games? By showing up at a place that only holds good memories for me?" I gesture to the shimmering lake, its surface reflecting the clear blue sky, and it feels like a cruel reminder of what we once had.

He takes a breath, his expression serious now. "I didn't come here to mess with you. I came to warn you."

"Warn me?" My brow furrows as curiosity seeps into my anger. "About what?"

"About someone who's watching you."

A chill runs down my spine, icy tendrils wrapping around my heart. "What do you mean? Who?"

"I can't say too much, but you're not just dealing with the fallout of our past." He hesitates, and for a moment, uncertainty flickers across his features, but then he leans in closer, lowering his voice as if the trees themselves might overhear. "There are people who know about you—people who shouldn't."

"Are you serious?" My skepticism mingles with the rising anxiety curling in my stomach. "Why should I believe you? You're the one who disappeared!"

"I know," he replies, frustration lining his voice. "But you have to trust me on this. I didn't just find you by chance; I came because I've been looking out for you. There's a reason I called you last night."

"Then why not just say it? Why the cryptic messages?"

"Because it's complicated," he sighs, running a hand through his tousled hair, a gesture that feels achingly familiar. "I needed to gauge your reaction, to see if you'd even want to listen to me again. I had to make sure you were safe before I exposed anything further."

"Safe from what?"

His eyes dart away for a moment, as if he's weighing his options. "From someone who thinks they can use your past against you. I don't know the details, but they've been looking for you."

The words settle heavily in the air, a suffocating weight I can hardly process. "Who?" I demand, fear creeping into my voice.

"I can't tell you yet," he says, his expression tight. "But trust me, you need to be careful. The more you dig into the past, the more dangerous it becomes. And I don't want you to get hurt."

A myriad of emotions swirls within me—anger, fear, confusion. "And you think showing up here like some sort of dark knight in shining armor is supposed to help? What exactly do you plan to do, Ethan?"

He leans in, his intensity igniting a fire within me, the tension crackling like electricity. "I'm here to protect you, Lexi. I made a mistake before, but I won't make it again. I'm not leaving you to face this alone."

"Why should I trust you?"

"Because," he says softly, "despite everything, I still care about you. I never stopped."

My heart lurches at his confession, caught in a storm of emotions I can't seem to untangle. The space between us thickens, and for a moment, it feels as if the world outside has faded away, leaving only the two of us suspended in this fragile moment.

Just then, a rustling sound breaks the tension, pulling us back to reality. I spin toward the noise, my heart racing, and see a shadow darting between the trees. My breath hitches, and I take a step back, instinctively reaching for Ethan. "Did you see that?"

He nods, his expression shifting to one of concern. "Stay close."

The world narrows to the sound of our breathing and the low rustle of the underbrush, anxiety tightening around us like a vice. The moment feels charged, fraught with unspoken words and hidden dangers, and as I glance back at Ethan, uncertainty lingers in the air.

I'm about to ask what we should do next when a figure emerges from the shadows—tall, broad-shouldered, with an aura that feels both familiar and menacing. My breath catches in my throat as recognition washes over me like icy water.

"Ethan," I whisper, the fear in my voice trembling on the edge of disbelief. "Who is that?"

Ethan's face pales, the confident facade crumbling as he mutters a single word, his eyes widening in horror. "Run."

Chapter 7: A Reunion of Lies

I can't take it anymore. I need answers. The gnawing in my gut pulls me toward him, each step an uneasy reminder of every unspoken word and forgotten promise. The day is blisteringly hot, and the air hangs heavy with the scent of freshly baked bread from the nearby bakery, a place I often frequented with Ethan. I've walked this street so many times, and yet, the thought that he's been just a few blocks away—living, breathing, thriving—makes my skin crawl.

The neighborhood hums around me, people bustling about, immersed in their own lives, their own secrets. I can feel the weight of my intentions pressing against me like a leaden cloak, suffocating and inescapable. I finally reach his apartment building, a nondescript structure that I can't believe has housed him all this time. A strange sense of déjà vu washes over me, as if I'm returning to a long-lost childhood home where the echoes of laughter mingle with shadows of heartache.

The hallway smells faintly of lemon-scented cleaner and stale pizza, a combination that conjures memories of late-night conversations, where time melted away with every slice and every laugh. I lift my hand to knock, hesitating just long enough to hear the faint thud of my heart. It's ridiculous, this fear, yet it's real. He's the one who left, after all, and now I'm the one on his doorstep.

With a deep breath, I rap my knuckles against the door, a timid sound that belies the tempest swirling inside me. When the door swings open, the sight of him momentarily steals my breath. Ethan stands there, tousled hair falling into his eyes, an old T-shirt clinging to his frame in that effortless way I used to find so attractive. But it's the surprise etched on his face that catches me off guard, the way his eyes widen, a flicker of something—regret, perhaps?—flashing before it vanishes like smoke in the wind.

"Hey," I manage, my voice barely more than a whisper. "We need to talk."

He looks taken aback, caught between the mundane reality of a Wednesday afternoon and the whirlwind of emotions he's clearly avoided for far too long. "I wasn't expecting—"

"Clearly," I cut him off, pushing past him into the familiar chaos of his apartment. The walls, once adorned with our memories, now feel like a gallery of ghosts. Pizza boxes and laundry conspire with dust bunnies in a strange dance of neglect, and I suddenly want to shake him for letting everything slip away like this.

"Can we sit?" he asks, his voice a mix of hesitation and something softer, something that makes my heart race and my mind spin.

I nod, letting him guide me to the couch, which feels like a relic of our past, worn but cozy. I sink into its depths, the fabric familiar yet foreign, like stepping into a dream that's lost its magic. He hovers nearby, unsure whether to sit beside me or across the room as if distance might somehow dull the impact of this reunion. The air thickens with unspoken words, and I can almost hear the ticking of the clock, counting down the moments until I either get what I need or leave this place with nothing but more questions.

"You said you needed to talk?" he prompts, his tone casual but the tension palpable.

"Yeah." I lean forward, my heart pounding like a drum in my chest. "Why didn't you tell me you were back in town? You've been living just a few blocks away, Ethan. How could you just... hide?"

A flicker of something shifts in his expression, and for a brief moment, I think I see the vulnerability beneath his bravado. "I didn't think you wanted to see me," he finally says, his voice low and almost pleading. "After everything..."

"Everything?" I scoff, frustration boiling beneath the surface. "You mean the way you just walked away? The lies? I deserve more than vague answers, Ethan. I deserve the truth."

He leans back, crossing his arms defensively, and I can see the walls he's built around himself, brick by brick, fortified by years of silence. "I haven't been listening to your show," he starts, but I can hear the cracks in his voice, the fissures in his carefully constructed façade. "I didn't call in."

"Really?" I challenge, raising an eyebrow. "Because I thought I heard your voice the other day. Someone called in asking about betrayal, asking how to move on. Sounded a lot like you."

His eyes dart away, and I can almost see the gears turning in his head, wrestling with honesty and self-preservation. "I... I don't know what to say," he admits, and I can see it—his reluctance to dive into the deep end with me, to untangle the mess we created together.

"Try the truth," I urge, feeling a rush of desperation. "Did you think I'd just forget? That I wouldn't care? You're acting like I'm some stranger."

"Maybe that's what I wanted," he mutters, almost to himself, but the words hit me like a slap. The reality of his admission sinks in, leaving me reeling. I can't decide whether to be angry or heartbroken or both.

"Ethan," I start, the weight of his admission heavy on my tongue, "you don't get to play games with me anymore. I'm done pretending that everything is fine."

He looks at me then, truly looks, and in his gaze, I see the fear—fear of what we once were, fear of what we could never be again. "It's not that simple," he murmurs, voice thick with unarticulated feelings. "You think you know me, but I've changed."

"Changed? Or just run away?" I counter, a sharpness creeping into my voice. "Because the last time I checked, you left me without so much as a goodbye. You don't get to rewrite our history because it's convenient for you."

Silence hangs heavy between us, the words suspended in the air like a storm cloud, threatening to burst at any moment. I can almost feel the pulse of the room as we stand on the precipice of something real, something raw, and terrifying. He opens his mouth to speak, but I know better than to let him fill the space with empty reassurances.

I want to shake him, to make him understand the gravity of what he's done, how he's turned my life upside down with his absence. And yet, a part of me yearns to bridge the chasm between us, to find the remnants of the connection we once shared.

The silence stretches like an elastic band between us, taut with unspoken tension. I can see his jaw tighten, a muscle flickering as he struggles for composure. This isn't just a reunion; it feels like standing on the edge of a cliff, the wind howling around us, daring us to leap. I can't shake the feeling that beneath his casual demeanor lies a storm, and I'm desperate to know if he's ready to face it.

"Why now?" I press, leaning in closer, my voice dropping to a whisper, as if the very walls could eavesdrop on our revelations. "Why not reach out when you first came back? What's kept you away all this time?"

Ethan's expression falters. For a brief moment, his mask slips, revealing a glimpse of vulnerability that makes my heart lurch. "I didn't think you'd want to see me," he admits, his gaze dropping to the floor as if he's suddenly become more interested in the worn carpet than the conversation we're having.

"Maybe I wouldn't have, but you didn't even give me the chance," I say, my frustration bubbling to the surface. "Instead, you let me wonder, let me assume I was abandoned without so much as a word."

He looks up then, his eyes intense, filled with a mix of emotions that mirror my own. "You don't understand," he says, and there's a rawness in his tone that cuts through the air like a knife. "I was trying to protect you."

"Protect me? By disappearing?" The incredulity in my voice is palpable. "I don't need your protection, Ethan. I need honesty, even if it hurts. Just tell me why you've been so close yet so far."

He runs a hand through his hair, a nervous habit I remember all too well. "Because sometimes the truth is scarier than silence," he replies, his voice dropping to a whisper, as if he fears the walls might betray him, too.

"Scary?" I echo, my anger flaring. "Try living in the dark for years, wondering if the person you loved was dead or alive. That's scary."

His eyes soften, a glimmer of remorse shining through the haze of confusion. "I never wanted to hurt you," he says, his voice barely above a murmur. "But I thought you'd be better off without me. I thought... I thought I was doing the right thing."

"Doing the right thing?" I scoff, disbelief dripping from my words. "You don't get to decide what's best for me. That's my choice, not yours."

Ethan shifts uncomfortably, the weight of my words clearly settling on his shoulders. "I know, I know. I messed up. But I had my reasons. Things got complicated."

"Complicated?" I repeat, my eyebrows arching in skepticism. "Complicated how? You can't drop that bombshell and expect me to just nod along like it's a normal Tuesday afternoon."

He exhales sharply, frustration flickering in his eyes. "There are things I haven't told you, things that I wasn't ready to share. And now—"

"Now you think it's all okay because you decided to show up?" I interrupt, incredulity mixing with the growing sense of betrayal. "You can't just walk in here after years and expect me to be all warm and fuzzy. You think I'm just going to fall back into your arms?"

"No," he replies quickly, desperation creeping into his voice. "I don't expect anything. I just... I want to explain. To make you understand."

My heart beats loudly in my chest, a steady rhythm of hope and skepticism. "Then do it," I challenge. "But know that I won't take half-truths or excuses. You either lay it all out or we're done here."

He sighs, running a hand down his face as if bracing himself for impact. "Okay," he concedes, his tone shifting from defensive to contemplative. "When I left, it was because I was caught up in something I didn't know how to get out of. There were... complications with my family."

I arch an eyebrow, intrigued despite myself. "Complications? What does that even mean? Are we talking family drama or something more sinister?"

"Both, I guess." He leans back, vulnerability flashing across his features. "My parents were in a bad place, fighting constantly. It was like living in a war zone. I didn't know how to handle it, and I thought leaving would be better for everyone."

"Better for everyone?" I can't hide the incredulity in my voice. "You thought abandoning me was better? Do you even hear yourself?"

"I was afraid!" he bursts out, his frustration spilling over. "Afraid of what it meant to stay, afraid I'd drag you down with me. You deserved happiness, and I couldn't give it to you."

His admission hits me like a punch to the gut. The raw honesty in his words cuts through my anger, but I refuse to let him see how deeply he affects me. "So, you thought you'd spare me by ghosting? That's not how love works, Ethan."

He flinches at the word love, and I can see the wheels turning in his mind as if he's trying to navigate the minefield we've created between us. "I know that now. But back then, I was just a kid trying to find his way in a world that was falling apart. I didn't think you'd want to be part of my chaos."

My heart softens a fraction, but the frustration remains. "So, what? You thought if you just vanished, I'd magically heal? That I wouldn't wonder what happened to you? You're wrong."

"Maybe," he admits, his voice barely above a whisper. "But the truth is, I missed you. I miss us. I thought I could just move on, but it's not that simple."

"Tell me what you want, Ethan," I urge, the desperation creeping into my tone. "Because right now, I feel like I'm talking to a stranger in your old skin."

He takes a breath, his gaze steady on mine, and for the first time, I see a flicker of resolve. "I want to make things right. I want to explain everything, even the parts that scare me."

I lean forward, the air between us crackling with anticipation. "Then do it. But know that this isn't just about you. This is about us—what we had and what we could still have. And I refuse to go back to the shadows."

He nods, and for a brief moment, I think he's ready to lay it all on the line. But just then, the sound of a muffled ringtone cuts through the tension, vibrating ominously from his pocket. He reaches for it, his expression shifting to one of discomfort. "I need to get this," he says, his voice suddenly distant, the intimacy of our moment slipping away.

"Really? Now?" I cross my arms, irritation boiling up again.

"Just a second," he insists, pulling the phone from his pocket, his eyes darting to the screen. I watch as his expression hardens, a flicker of panic flashing in his gaze.

"Ethan?" I ask, my heart racing as he steps away, his voice lowering into a tense murmur. Whatever is happening is not good, and the feeling in my gut is turning ominous. I can barely hear his side of the conversation, but the tension radiates off him, thick enough to slice through.

"I'll handle it," he says, a tone I don't like. "Just stay out of it."

I rise, the unease settling like ice in my veins. "Ethan, what's going on?"

But he just shakes his head, his focus on the call. The moment we were sharing fades, replaced by an undercurrent of danger that seeps into the air between us. And as he steps back, leaving me standing there, I can't shake the feeling that this is just the beginning of another twist in our already tangled story.

Chapter 8: Dangerous Connections

I traced my fingers over the coffee-stained paper spread out before me, a chaotic array of notes and half-formed thoughts that felt like a maze with no exit. The dim light from the overhead bulb flickered as if it, too, was questioning my sanity. The walls of my tiny apartment closed in, filled with the remnants of old pizza boxes and a sea of brightly colored Post-it notes that once served as reminders of happier days—days before I became ensnared in this tangled web of secrets and lies.

Ethan, my once-loyal friend, now loomed like a shadow in my mind. The way he'd backed away after that last phone call, his eyes darting as if he had seen a ghost, stirred an uneasy flutter in my chest. But it wasn't just him. As the sun sank behind the high rises outside my window, casting long shadows that danced across my floor, I began to unravel the unsettling truth: there were others. The realization hit me like a slap, a stinging wake-up call echoing through my thoughts.

It started as whispers during the livestreams, comments that seemed innocent at first, sweet nothings wrapped in enthusiasm for my quirky sense of humor. "Love your show! You're the highlight of my day!" they'd say, but now those words felt like bait. Each one a hook waiting to reel me into deeper waters. I could almost hear their voices ringing in my ears, echoing in a sinister symphony that played every time I closed my eyes. It was as if my life had morphed into a cheap thriller, and I was the lead character who had unwittingly walked into a trap.

I rubbed my temples, trying to dispel the mounting tension as I picked up my phone to scroll through comments from the latest episode. There it was—a familiar username, one I'd seen countless times before, but its presence now sent a shiver down my spine. "You should be careful, Claire. Not everyone who watches is a fan." The message was innocuous enough, but the implication curled my stomach into knots. How had they known that I was feeling paranoid? The way the letters sprawled across the screen, taunting me, felt like a silent scream echoing in a darkened room.

In a flash, my thoughts darted back to Ellie, my partner in crime and co-host. Could she be involved? We had laughed, shared dreams, and tackled the absurdity of our lives together. Yet, a seed of doubt sprouted in my mind. What if she was in on this twisted game? What if, behind those expressive eyes and her ready smile, she was hiding something darker? The very idea felt like shards of glass in my chest, painfully sharp yet oddly intoxicating.

"Hey, Claire!" Ellie's voice chimed from the kitchen, breaking through my spiraling thoughts. "Do you want to grab dinner? I was thinking tacos from that place you love." She appeared around the corner, her hair a wild halo of curls, glowing in the soft light of our grimy kitchen. She was my sun, always brightening the day, but today, even her sunshine felt filtered through a cloud of suspicion.

I hesitated, weighing the prospect of her inviting me out against the backdrop of my fears. "Sure," I finally said, forcing a smile that felt more like a grimace. "Tacos sound great."

As we walked to the little Mexican joint down the street, the air buzzed with the promise of cool evening breezes and the laughter of people spilling out of bars and cafes. I inhaled the familiar scent of grilled meat and spices wafting through the air, a welcome distraction from the chaos of my mind. But with every step, I couldn't shake the feeling that someone was watching us, lurking just out of sight.

"Everything okay?" Ellie asked, her brows knitted together in that way that always made me feel seen. "You seem a little... off."

I shrugged, the weight of my secrets pressing down on me. "Just tired, I guess. Work has been crazy." I couldn't meet her eyes, afraid she might see through my carefully constructed facade.

She took a sip of her drink, her expression unreadable. "You know you can talk to me about anything, right? Like, if something's bothering you, I can help."

The sincerity in her voice cut through my apprehension. I thought about confessing everything—the caller, the ominous messages, my fears. But what if her reaction confirmed my worst fears? What if she laughed, called me paranoid, and assured me I was overreacting? The battle raged in my mind, tugging me in two different directions, but ultimately, my mouth sealed tighter than a vault.

"Really, I'm fine," I said, forcing a laugh that sounded more like a bark. "Just hungry."

The tension lingered like a shadow as we settled into our seats at the restaurant, the vibrant decor a stark contrast to the gray clouds swirling inside my head. We munched on tacos piled high with colorful toppings, the flavors bursting in my mouth while my thoughts churned like a storm. Ellie chattered about her day, animatedly gesturing with her hands, but I couldn't focus. My gaze kept flicking toward the door, expecting someone to burst through, an ominous figure that might unravel my entire life.

A sudden clatter made me jump, a nearby table of diners erupting in laughter, oblivious to my turmoil. I glanced back at Ellie, who was mid-story, her laughter infectious but hollow to my ears. She reached across the table, squeezing my hand, her warmth providing a flicker of comfort in my growing dread.

"Seriously, Claire," she said, her voice low and earnest. "If something's wrong, you have to tell me. You're scaring me a little."

Her concern hung in the air, palpable and heavy. I opened my mouth to respond, but the words got lost in the tangled web of fear and doubt. The restaurant felt smaller, the walls closing in, as I searched for the right thing to say. But the only sound that escaped was a whisper, barely audible above the bustling chatter around us. "I don't know who to trust anymore."

"I don't know who to trust anymore." The words slipped from my lips, heavy and soaked in dread, hanging between us like a thunderstorm ready to unleash its fury. Ellie's grip tightened around my hand, her expression shifting from concern to something resembling determination.

"What do you mean?" she pressed, the easy cadence of her voice now edged with urgency. "Did something happen? Is it about the show?"

I swallowed hard, feeling the weight of my truth. "It's just... I've been getting these calls. Strange messages. It feels like someone's been watching me." The admission clung to the air, each syllable tinged with the weight of fear I had tried to dismiss for too long.

Ellie's brow furrowed, and for a fleeting moment, I saw a flicker of disbelief in her eyes. But it was quickly replaced by the fierce loyalty that made her my rock. "Okay, we'll figure this out together," she declared, her tone resolute as she flagged down the waiter for another round of drinks, the clinking of glasses an awkward reminder of our surroundings.

As we sipped our margaritas, I watched her closely, hoping to catch a hint of deception, some sign that she was in on whatever game was being played. But Ellie was nothing if not genuine, and the fire in her eyes only fueled my desire to trust her.

"Do you remember that creepy message you got last week?" she asked, her expression shifting to one of concern as she leaned closer. "You should've told me then. It's not something to brush off."

I chuckled weakly, trying to lighten the mood despite the heaviness that still clung to me. "Oh, you mean the one where they claimed I was 'the light of their day'? So sweet, right?"

"Definitely not sweet. More like a horror movie waiting to happen." She shook her head, hair bouncing with the motion. "You need to take this seriously. What did the caller say?"

The memory flooded back—his low voice slithering through the phone like a serpent, dark and unsettling. "He mentioned things only someone close to me would know," I confessed. "My childhood pet, the time I slipped on the ice in front of that coffee shop last winter... How does he know those things? It feels like my life has become a script for a thriller I never signed up for."

Ellie's eyes darkened with worry, and I felt the ground beneath me shift. "We should go to the police. This isn't just a prank; it's threatening. You need to protect yourself."

I nodded but felt the trepidation bubble up again. The police would probably roll their eyes and chalk it up to paranoia, a lonely woman trying to make sense of a confusing world. What could I possibly prove? But as the thought lingered, the tension in my chest coiled tighter. "You're right. I'll report it tomorrow."

With the plan set, I felt a semblance of relief wash over me, though the creeping shadow of dread still loomed. I changed the subject, forcing a grin as I teased Ellie about her love life. "So, did you ever text that cute bartender back?"

Her laughter rang like a bell, but the forced nature of it tugged at my heart. "Maybe I'm waiting for you to play matchmaker," she shot back, her playful tone barely disguising her worry. "I need to know you're okay first."

We continued to banter, and for a moment, the world outside melted away, replaced by laughter and shared memories. The laughter felt hollow, though, like a flimsy wall built against a rising tide. I could feel the tension beneath the surface, a current of unspoken fears threading through our lighthearted conversation.

Later that night, after we returned home, I sank into my couch, the soft cushions enveloping me like a blanket of safety. But the sense of security was fleeting, the gnawing anxiety creeping back as I turned on my laptop, the glow illuminating the dark corners of my thoughts.

As I began to sift through the messages from viewers, searching for any thread that might lead me closer to understanding who was behind the ominous calls, my heart raced. Each comment was like a needle in a haystack, each name a potential lead, but no clues emerged. Just the same fandom enthusiasm, endless emojis, and compliments that suddenly felt like a disguise.

Then, amidst the sea of supportive words, I spotted it again—a new comment from that familiar username, the one that had sparked my initial paranoia. "You're doing great, Claire. Just remember, not everyone has your best interests at heart."

Chills raced down my spine, and I felt my pulse quicken. It was the same tone, the same eerie undertone that had haunted me before. My fingers hovered over the keyboard as I debated whether to respond, whether to provoke whatever dark force lay behind that username. But fear anchored me in place, the risk of exposing myself too great.

Before I could second-guess my instincts, my phone buzzed beside me. I picked it up, heart hammering in my chest. It was a text from an unknown number, the message simple yet unnerving: "We need to talk."

My skin prickled with dread as the realization struck: the game was escalating, and I was in the center of a storm that was growing more unpredictable by the moment. I hesitated, fingers trembling over the screen as I debated whether to respond or ignore it entirely. But the sense of urgency, the need to uncover the truth, propelled me forward.

"Who is this?" I typed, my heart racing as I hit send. The seconds felt like hours as I waited, the silence echoing around me. Then, almost immediately, the reply came through: "You know exactly who I am, Claire. But it's time you understood the bigger picture."

I leaned back, heart pounding as the room closed in around me. Suddenly, my phone buzzed again, this time ringing with an incoming call. I hesitated, recognizing the number as the one that had haunted my dreams for weeks. I knew I should ignore it; I knew I should just turn off my phone and bury myself in a sea of distraction. But something inside me—an insatiable curiosity mixed with fear—urged me to answer.

With trembling hands, I accepted the call, heart racing as the familiar voice slid into my ear like a whisper in the dark. "I've been waiting for you to pick up."

Chapter 9: The Fall of Walls

The moon hung low that night, a colossal pearl spilling silver light across the cracks in the pavement, illuminating the world in shades of ethereal blue. I was sprawled across my couch, clutching a half-empty bottle of red wine and flipping through an old photo album. The faded images tugged at my heart, each picture a fragment of the life I used to know—hazy summers filled with laughter and the kind of love that ignited every room. But as I turned the pages, the warmth slipped away, leaving behind a cool reminder of everything I had lost.

It was the kind of evening that felt haunted by ghosts, where every creak of the floorboards whispered tales of what once was. My little apartment, with its mismatched furniture and curtains that swayed like delicate ballerinas, felt too small for the weight of my memories. I glanced at the clock; the ticking seemed louder than usual, counting down to something I couldn't quite place.

I took another swig of wine, relishing the burn as it coursed down my throat. Just as I was about to lose myself in yet another memory of when love was uncomplicated, my phone buzzed violently against the coffee table, its screen illuminating the dark like a flare.

I picked it up, squinting at the name that flashed before me: Ethan. My stomach did a little dance, a twisted combination of dread and exhilaration. Ethan was a paradox wrapped in charm and sarcasm, always managing to find his way back into my life just when I thought I had firmly closed the door.

"Hey," I said, my voice slightly hoarse from the wine.

"Is this a bad time?" His voice oozed that familiar blend of confidence and mischief, like a favorite song that brings both joy and a tinge of regret.

I hesitated. "Not really. I was just—"

"Great! I'm outside."

The way he said it sent a shiver down my spine. I shot up from the couch, nearly toppling over as I rushed to the window. Sure enough, there he was, leaning against his motorcycle, the streetlights casting shadows that danced around him. I hadn't seen him in months, and yet there he stood, just as I remembered: dark hair tousled, a teasing smile that could disarm even the most resolute heart, and an air of danger that was all his own.

"Seriously? You just show up?" I muttered to myself, torn between annoyance and the undeniable thrill of seeing him again.

Without giving it much thought, I swung open the door, the wood creaking like it had something to say about my decision.

"What are you doing here, Ethan?" I tried to sound stern, but the words felt weak, the way I felt when I was around him.

He stepped inside, brushing past me, and I caught a whiff of leather and something distinctly him—maybe sandalwood or maybe just trouble. "Thought I'd surprise you. Miss me?"

I rolled my eyes, crossing my arms defensively. "Oh, absolutely. Just what I needed tonight."

His grin widened, lighting up his angular features, and my resolve began to dissolve like sugar in warm tea. "You're lying, and you know it."

Before I could muster a response, he plopped down on the couch, the springs creaking in protest. He picked up the bottle of wine, eyeing it like it was an old friend. "Mind if I?"

"Fine. But just one glass." I felt like I was negotiating a treaty with a particularly charming enemy.

He poured himself a generous amount, then leaned back, his gaze piercing yet playful. "You look good, by the way. Still rocking the 'I don't care' vibe?"

"Thanks," I muttered, the corners of my mouth twitching despite my best efforts. "And it's called being comfortable."

"Right. Let's go with that." He took a sip, his eyes narrowing slightly as he savored the wine. "So, tell me about your boring life, Amelia."

"Boring? You have no idea." I launched into a retelling of my days filled with work, writing, and the occasional existential crisis. He listened, nodding along, his expression shifting from amusement to a deeper, contemplative gaze.

But then came the moment that shifted everything. The conversation flowed naturally until I mentioned my latest article, a piece exploring the nuances of love and loss. As I spoke, I noticed Ethan's expression darkening, the lightness slipping away as if a cloud had passed over the moon.

"You really think you understand it all?" he asked, his voice low and serious.

I paused, taken aback by the sudden change in tone. "What do you mean?"

He leaned forward, elbows resting on his knees, eyes locked onto mine with a fierce intensity. "Love isn't just a story you write about. It's messy, complicated, and sometimes it hurts more than you can imagine."

The air crackled between us, and I couldn't tell if it was tension or an electric connection that ignited the space. "I know it can be difficult," I countered softly, "but that doesn't mean we shouldn't try."

"Trying doesn't always lead to happy endings, Amelia," he replied, the weight of his words hanging like a dense fog.

As if on cue, a loud crash reverberated outside, jolting us both from the moment. I darted toward the window, my heart racing, but all I saw was a shadow darting down the alley, disappearing into the night.

"What was that?" Ethan asked, standing abruptly, his demeanor shifting back to the playful teasing I had come to expect.

"Just... a noise," I replied, trying to shake off the feeling that something was lurking just beyond my view. But the unease settled in my stomach like a stone, refusing to budge.

"Let me check it out," he offered, slipping into a more protective role.

"No! You can't just—"

Before I could finish my sentence, he was already out the door, the weight of his presence vanishing into the night. I stood there, torn between concern and frustration, caught in the undertow of a conversation that had ventured far beyond the walls I had built.

It was then that I realized how easy it was for him to step back in, to pull me from the shadows of my own making and into a world filled with unpredictability. But I was not ready for the tide of memories, feelings, and truths that might come crashing down around us.

I stood frozen in the doorway, my heart pounding in my chest like a trapped bird. The cool night air rushed in, mingling with the warmth of my apartment and carrying with it the faint scent of rain and something metallic that made my stomach twist. I peered out into the dark, but Ethan had vanished into the shadows like a wisp of smoke, and an uneasy knot formed in my gut.

"Ethan?" I called, my voice sounding small against the stillness. No reply. The world outside felt charged, electric, as if it were holding its breath, waiting for something to happen. I took a step outside, the pavement cold under my bare feet, and strained my ears to catch any sound. But the only thing I heard was the soft rustle of leaves, whispering secrets that I wasn't quite ready to uncover.

I turned back to the apartment, half-tempted to slam the door and barricade myself from whatever chaos awaited me out there. But there was something about Ethan that made my heart race, a reckless desire to unravel the threads of his unpredictable charm. I stepped forward, and just as I reached the edge of the stoop, I heard a scuffle followed by a muffled curse.

"Ethan!" Panic shot through me, and I rushed down the steps, my instincts kicking in despite the protest of my rational mind. He needed me—or maybe I needed him. The streetlight flickered ominously, casting a flickering glow that danced across the pavement.

I rounded the corner of the building and caught sight of him grappling with a shadowy figure, the two of them twisting and turning in a clash of wills. My heart sank as I watched the struggle unfold, caught between the urge to run away and the instinct to rush in.

"Let go of him!" I shouted, surprising even myself with the ferocity in my voice. My feet took me closer, and before I could stop myself, I was within shouting distance, adrenaline surging through my veins.

Ethan's head whipped around, surprise etching his features for just a moment before he turned back to his opponent, a man cloaked in darkness, his features obscured. "Amelia, get back!"

But it was too late. I wasn't about to retreat; instead, I charged forward, ready to do something—anything—to help. The air was thick with tension, and every instinct screamed that I was stepping into a danger I couldn't comprehend.

Just as I lunged, the man threw a punch, and Ethan dodged with a grace that surprised me. My stomach lurched as the shadowy figure stumbled back, momentarily disoriented, but not defeated.

"Stay out of this!" Ethan barked, but I couldn't hear him over the pounding of my heart, echoing in my ears. I was here, and I wasn't going anywhere.

I glanced around, looking for something, anything, to use as a weapon. A nearby trash can caught my eye. Desperation fueled my actions as I grabbed the lid and brandished it like a shield, adrenaline coursing through me as I shouted, "Hey! Leave him alone!"

The figure turned, startled by my sudden appearance. He hesitated just long enough for Ethan to regain his footing. "Amelia, no!" he yelled again, but the words barely reached me.

The man shifted, his expression morphing from surprise to anger, his eyes glinting with a feral intensity. "You shouldn't have come out here, girl."

I clenched my jaw, refusing to back down. "You don't scare me."

With that, I swung the lid with all my might. It connected with the man's shoulder, causing him to grunt in pain. Ethan seized the moment, pushing the figure back hard enough that he stumbled, giving me a fleeting sense of victory. But it was short-lived as the man regained his composure, eyes narrowing like a predator sizing up its prey.

"Nice move, Amelia," Ethan said, a flicker of admiration cutting through the tension. "But you need to—"

"I said, get back!" I shot back, feeling a surge of defiance. I wasn't just some damsel waiting to be rescued; I was in this too, whether he liked it or not.

The man's lip curled into a sneer as he eyed us both. "You're making a mistake." His voice was gravelly, laced with a threat that hung heavily in the air.

Suddenly, he lunged toward Ethan, and my heart dropped. Time slowed as I watched the two of them collide. Ethan ducked and twisted, narrowly avoiding a punch, but the figure wasn't just fighting; he was looking for something.

"Ethan, watch out!" I yelled, lunging forward once more, the lid still in my grip.

But before I could reach him, the man pulled out something shiny from his pocket—a knife. My breath caught in my throat, the world narrowing down to that glinting blade that seemed to capture the very essence of danger.

"Get down!" Ethan shouted, and I didn't need to be told twice. I dropped to the ground just as he pushed the assailant away, the two of them grappling for control, wrestling in a dance of survival.

I could hear the scrape of feet on the pavement, the heavy breathing punctuated by grunts of effort. Fear gripped me like a vise as I scrambled to my feet again, searching desperately for anything that could tip the scales.

"Stop this!" I shouted, hoping my voice would somehow shatter the tension, but it only drew the figure's attention. He turned toward me, and in that split second, I realized he was calculating his next move.

Ethan seized the opportunity and twisted, knocking the knife from the man's grip, but that just made him angrier. The blade clattered to the ground, a stark reminder of how close we were to something truly terrible.

I grabbed Ethan's arm, pulling him back as the man lunged for the knife. "We can't let him get it!"

Ethan's eyes were intense, his jaw set with determination. "We need to get out of here."

"Where?" I glanced around frantically, feeling the urgency of the moment clawing at my sanity.

"Inside!" He grabbed my hand, yanking me back toward the safety of my apartment.

Just as we turned, the man lunged again, and I heard the whoosh of air as he barely missed my arm. A sharp gasp escaped my lips as I felt the rush of danger. I barely managed to pull the door closed behind us, slamming it shut as adrenaline surged through me, making my limbs shake.

We were safe—at least for now—but the night was far from over. I pressed my back against the door, breathless, my heart racing in rhythm with the chaos outside. "What the hell was that?"

Ethan's eyes were wide, his expression a mix of frustration and urgency. "I don't know, but we need to figure it out—now."

But just as he reached for the door to ensure it was locked, a loud crash echoed from outside, and the unmistakable sound of shattering glass filled the air. My heart plummeted as dread coiled tightly in my stomach.

"Get back!" I whispered urgently, the walls of my sanctuary suddenly feeling like a fragile bubble about to burst.

Ethan turned, his face a mask of resolve, but I could see the uncertainty swirling beneath it. The storm wasn't just outside anymore; it was creeping in, and there was no telling what would happen next.

Chapter 10: Behind the Mask

A chill wraps around me, squeezing my lungs tight. I can't shake the sensation that the shadows in my room are more than just darkness; they are alive, pulsating with a heartbeat that mirrors my own. Each tick of the clock echoes in my mind, a reminder that time is slipping away, and with it, the thin veneer of safety I cling to. What kind of person lingers in the hallways, silently observing, waiting for an opening? The thought unnerves me, gnawing at the edges of my thoughts like a restless mouse searching for crumbs.

My phone buzzes on the nightstand, breaking the silence with a sharp jolt. I snatch it up, heart racing, expecting the caller's name to light up the screen. Instead, it's just a notification from my favorite online shop, tempting me with the latest seasonal trends. I toss the phone back onto the bedside table, the movement fueled by frustration and anxiety, and bury my face in the pillows. The plush fabric wraps around me, cocooning me in a fabric embrace that feels more like a tomb than a refuge.

I toss and turn, desperately trying to find a comfortable position, but the fear keeps me tossing like a ship caught in a storm. Images of the figure flood my mind, his silhouette sharp against the glow of the hallway lights, the way his presence felt like a dark cloud creeping closer. He was there—so close—but then he vanished, just like that, leaving behind a whirlpool of questions and a creeping sense of dread.

Morning comes with a dull light spilling through the window, and the world seems eerily normal. I force myself out of bed, still haunted by the memory of that night. Breakfast feels like a chore; I mechanically toast bread, watching the uneven browning of the edges, lost in thought. "You're awfully quiet this morning," Ellie chirps as she breezes into the kitchen, her presence like a splash of sunshine in my otherwise dreary morning.

I manage a weak smile, swirling the coffee in my mug, the steam curling up like tiny ghosts disappearing into the air. "Just tired, I guess," I mumble, knowing full well I can't share the truth. How do you explain to your best friend that you're being stalked by a shadowy figure who calls you at odd hours, weaving your life into some surreal tapestry of anxiety? It sounds ridiculous, even to my own ears.

"Maybe we should hit the café later, get some pastries? You could use a sugar rush," she suggests, her eyes sparkling with enthusiasm. The idea feels like a lifeline, a chance to escape the claustrophobic walls of my apartment and the lingering fear that stalks me. "Sure, why not?" I reply, my voice lighter than I feel. Perhaps the aroma of coffee and fresh pastries can wash away the unease, if only for a moment.

As the day progresses, I dive into my work, but my focus is shattered by thoughts of the figure. Each notification on my phone makes me jump, my heart skipping as I half-expect him to reveal himself through the screen. I keep glancing at the door, expecting it to swing open and him to step through, dark and brooding, like something out of a twisted fairy tale. My hands tremble as I type, fingers hovering above the keys, unsure if the world outside is safe or if it's just a façade hiding deeper dangers.

The café, with its bustling ambiance and the comforting chatter of patrons, feels like a temporary sanctuary. Ellie and I settle at our usual table, a cozy nook draped in fairy lights and surrounded by mismatched chairs that somehow feel like home. As I sip my latte, the warm liquid spreads through me, momentarily dulling my senses.

Ellie flips through her phone, occasionally glancing at me. "I swear you've been off lately. Is everything okay?" She leans forward, her brow furrowed with concern. I hesitate, the words forming in my mind but faltering on my tongue. I don't want to burden her with my fears, yet I can't pretend everything is fine.

"It's just work stuff. You know how it is," I say, plastering on a smile that feels as thin as the porcelain of my cup. She narrows her eyes, clearly not convinced. "Work stuff, huh? I see you practically living in the office."

"Someone has to keep the wheels turning," I reply, attempting to inject a lightness into my voice. "Besides, it's not like I have anything more interesting going on in my life."

"True, but you deserve a little fun. Maybe a night out? I heard about this great bar that's just opened up," she suggests, her excitement palpable. I feel the stirrings of a smile, but it's quickly swallowed by the weight of my anxiety. I glance toward the entrance, half-expecting to see him walking through the door, but instead, a gust of wind rushes in, sending a few napkins fluttering to the floor.

Just then, my phone buzzes, and I glance down. The caller ID reads "Unknown." My heart plummets. I exchange a glance with Ellie, her expression shifting from concern to alarm as she reads my face. The ringing continues, insistent and heavy, like the tolling of a bell marking my descent into chaos.

I swallow hard, my throat dry as I reach for the phone, the decision hanging heavy in the air. I can either answer and face whatever storm brews on the other side or let it linger, feeding my paranoia. The screen glows ominously in the café light, and I hesitantly swipe to answer, the sound of my pulse drumming in my ears drowning out everything else.

"Hello?" I say, trying to sound calm, but my voice trembles like a leaf caught in a breeze.

"Did you miss me?" The voice is smooth and dark, wrapping around my spine like cold fingers. My heart races, and I feel Ellie tense beside me, the weight of her gaze burning into my skin. I can't let fear consume me.

"What do you want?" I manage, my voice steadier than I feel.

"Oh, just wanted to see how you're doing behind the mask," he replies, his tone dripping with mockery. A chill creeps down my spine, a stark reminder that the shadows are alive, and I'm standing on the precipice of something terrifying.

"Did you miss me?" The voice cuts through the air like a knife, smooth and chilling. I feel the world around me fade, the café's warmth and chatter replaced by a stark, unforgiving silence. My mouth goes dry as I grip the phone tighter, the edges digging into my palm, and I catch a glimpse of Ellie's face, her eyes wide with a mix of concern and curiosity.

"What do you want?" I manage to choke out, forcing my voice to sound more confident than I feel.

"Oh, just checking in. It's been a while since we last talked, hasn't it?" He chuckles, the sound low and menacing, making the hairs on the back of my neck stand on end. "I figured you could use a friend. I must admit, I was worried you might be too scared to answer."

My heart races, a rapid drumbeat in my chest that threatens to drown out his words. "Why are you doing this?" I fire back, desperate to regain some semblance of control. The coffee shop feels like it's closing in on me, the vibrant colors blurring into a haze of anxiety.

"Doing what?" He feigns innocence, but there's a cruel edge to his voice that slices through the pretense. "I'm just here to help. After all, you have so much potential."

"Potential for what?" I ask, my tone sharp. "Are you stalking me now? What do you even want from me?" The truth is, the longer I keep him on the line, the more power he seems to hold over me, and that idea sends a wave of nausea rolling in my stomach.

"From you? It's not what I want, it's what you're afraid of. It's all those secrets you keep hidden behind that mask of yours," he replies, his voice silky smooth, like a serpent wrapping around its prey. "You can't hide forever, you know."

"Who says I'm hiding?" I snap, my voice rising a notch as a few patrons glance our way. My cheeks burn under their scrutiny, but I can't care about that now. The tension thickens, wrapping around us like a taut string ready to snap. "You're the one lurking in the shadows."

"I prefer to think of it as observing. You're far more interesting than the others," he says, and I can almost hear the smirk through the phone. "But let's not dwell on that. How about a little game?"

"A game?" I echo, my voice trembling.

"Precisely. A treasure hunt of sorts. If you play along, I'll give you the answers you're searching for. It's all in good fun, really."

"And if I refuse?"

"Ah, but that's where it gets interesting. You see, there are consequences for ignoring me." The sinister undertone sends chills racing down my spine.

Before I can respond, the connection drops with a finality that leaves me gasping for air, the silence ringing in my ears. Ellie reaches for my hand, grounding me back to reality. "What just happened? Who was that?"

"Someone I'd rather not have in my life," I reply, swallowing hard.

"Do you want me to call the cops?" Her concern is palpable, but I shake my head, unwilling to turn my life into a police procedural. I can't let fear dictate my actions, even if it feels like a heavy shadow clings to my every step.

"No, it's fine. I can handle this," I say, forcing a smile. "Maybe it's just a prank."

"Sure, if pranks involve psychological warfare," she mutters, her eyes narrowing. "But if you need to talk—"

"Really, Ellie. I'll be okay," I insist, brushing off her concern. It's not that I don't appreciate her worry; it's just that I'm terrified of dragging her into this. The last thing I want is to see her caught in the web of someone who thrives on chaos.

As we leave the café, the crisp air bites at my skin, a stark contrast to the warmth inside. I breathe deeply, trying to reclaim a sense of normalcy, but my mind drifts back to the figure, the voice, the hunt that has just begun. I need to make a plan, to outsmart him before he outsmarts me.

Later that night, I sit cross-legged on my bed, surrounded by notebooks and pens like a chaotic artist trying to make sense of the madness. My mind races, frantically scribbling down thoughts, ideas, and plans, each line blurring into the next. I need to gather every detail I can about this so-called game.

Suddenly, a soft knock on the door pulls me from my reverie. I glance at the clock—late for visitors. With a knot in my stomach, I approach the door, my heart pounding like a drum. "Who is it?"

"It's just me, Ellie!" she calls out, her voice bright and familiar. I crack the door open, and she barges in with a bag of snacks and an armful of movies. "I thought we could have a cozy night in and distract you from whatever that was earlier."

I feel a wave of gratitude wash over me, the tension in my shoulders easing. "You're a lifesaver, you know that?"

"Just trying to be the best best friend," she grins, dropping the bag on the floor and flopping onto my bed like it's the most comfortable couch in the world. "Now, how about we binge some terrible rom-coms? They always cheer me up."

I can't help but laugh, a genuine sound that feels foreign yet comforting. "You do know I'm not a fan of cliché, right?"

"Exactly why we're watching them. We need some bad acting to lighten the mood," she shoots back, her eyes sparkling with mischief.

The night unfolds with laughter, popcorn flying, and the gentle hum of background music, but a part of me remains restless, constantly aware of the unseen threat lurking just outside my door.

"Okay, but seriously," Ellie says during a pause, her voice dipping into seriousness. "What's the plan? You can't just ignore him."

I take a deep breath, the weight of the past hours crashing over me like a wave. "I need to play this game, Ellie. If I don't, I'm afraid of what he might do next."

"What do you mean by 'play'?"

"Find out what he wants, and figure out a way to turn it back on him."

Her eyes widen, a mix of admiration and concern flickering across her face. "You're playing with fire, you know that, right?"

"Maybe, but I can't let him dictate my life. I refuse to be scared."

As we dive into the movie once more, my phone buzzes again, and my stomach drops. It's another unknown number. I pick it up, my hands shaking, and as I glance at the screen, my breath hitches. The message reads: "Ready for the first clue? Let the hunt begin."

My heart races as I stare at the screen, the weight of his words heavy in the air. "What does it say?" Ellie asks, her curiosity piqued, but I can't bring myself to share the contents. I'm teetering on the edge of a cliff, and the ground beneath me is crumbling.

"Just something... unimportant," I murmur, my voice trembling as I try to keep the fear at bay. The night stretches before me like an ominous shadow, and I can't shake the feeling that the hunt is only beginning, the stakes higher than I ever imagined.

Chapter 11: Shattered Airwaves

The neon lights flicker like they're caught in a perpetual state of indecision, splashing shades of pink and blue across the cracked pavement as I dart through the alleyways. Each shadow feels like a ghost, but the truth is far scarier: it's not the dark that unnerves me; it's the lurking presence I can't quite shake. Every clatter of trash or rustle of wind sends a shiver skittering down my spine, but I refuse to give in to fear. Not now. I can't let it win.

I push open the door to my apartment, the familiar creak of the hinges a welcome sound amid the chaos in my mind. I stumble in, kicking off my shoes like they're anchors dragging me down. The small space is filled with the aroma of last week's takeout and a faint whiff of burnt coffee. It's a mess, but it's my mess, a sanctuary where I've constructed walls of comfort, however shabby they might be. I lean against the door, closing my eyes as I let the dim light wash over me like a gentle tide.

As I peel off my coat, I hear the unmistakable crunch of a crumpled takeout box beneath my foot. I glance down, and it hits me—this chaos isn't just around me; it's in me. I haven't just been dodging shadows outside; I've been battling demons inside, too. My thoughts race, a whirlwind of what-ifs and panic, and I drop onto the couch, the fabric cool against my skin. The only sound is the distant hum of traffic and the thudding of my heart, a reminder that I'm still alive, even if I feel like I'm barely hanging on.

Ellie had noticed something was off during the broadcast. Her concern had settled in my stomach like a rock, heavy and immovable. "You're not yourself," she'd said, her eyes wide and searching. How could I explain to her that my carefully constructed world felt like it was crumbling? That the voice that had once soared through airwaves now trembled with fear? I could almost hear the unspoken question hanging in the air: What's wrong with you?

But I'd smiled and deflected, the practiced performance rolling off my tongue like a well-worn script. "I'm fine," I'd chirped, like I believed it. I'd convinced myself that if I repeated the lie enough, it would turn into truth.

Now, sitting on my couch, I sift through my thoughts like I'm searching for a lost treasure. The recent events swirl in my mind, painting vivid scenes that pulse with urgency. The stranger with the piercing gaze, the shiver that crawled up my spine as I caught his reflection in a storefront window—every detail sharp and seared into my memory. It's like a gripping plot twist in one of those novels I used to devour. Except I'm the protagonist, and this isn't fiction.

I pull out my phone, staring at the screen as if it holds the answers to my questions. What am I supposed to do? Call the police? But for what? A feeling? A hunch? It sounds absurd even to my own ears. The truth is, I don't have any solid proof that anything is wrong, just a pervasive sense of dread that looms like a storm cloud, dark and looming.

The ticking clock on the wall becomes a metronome for my anxiety, each tick resonating like a countdown to some unknown catastrophe. I shove the phone aside, feeling its weightlessness. If I can't reach out to Ellie or anyone else, I can at least ground myself in the here and now. I lean back, focusing on the soothing rhythm of my breath, trying to let go of the turmoil inside.

Just as I start to find my center, a sudden knock on the door jolts me upright. My heart races, each thump echoing the fear that twists in my gut. Who could it be at this hour? I tiptoe toward the door, every step a mix of curiosity and dread. Peering through the peephole, I'm met with nothing but shadows in the hallway.

"Great, now I'm seeing things," I mutter under my breath. I swing the door open a crack, ready to confront whoever stands outside, my heart pounding like a drum.

To my surprise, it's a delivery person, hands tucked under their armpits to stave off the chill of the night air. "Package for you," they say, their breath fogging in the cool air.

"Oh, right!" I breathe, suddenly aware of how foolish I must look, half-dressed and frazzled. I take the package, its edges sharp against my fingertips. "Thank you."

As I shut the door, the relief washes over me in waves. But the moment I glance at the package, my heart sinks again. It's not just any delivery; it's a box marked with the logo of a company I once worked with, the glossy letters a stark reminder of a life I thought I'd left behind. My hands shake slightly as I pull the box to the couch, the curiosity gnawing at me like a hungry animal.

I tear into the packaging with a mix of anticipation and dread, and when I finally pull out the contents, it feels like unearthing a ghost from my past. Inside lies a stack of old scripts, my heart racing at the sight of the words I once poured my soul into. Flipping through them, the memories flood back—heady nights filled with creativity, laughter echoing in the dimly lit studio, and the camaraderie of a team that once felt like family. But alongside those memories is a gnawing sense of loss. Those days are long gone, buried under the weight of unfulfilled dreams and shadowy threats.

A slip of paper slips from the scripts, fluttering to the floor. I pick it up, my breath catching as I read the handwritten note: "You can't escape your past. It will always find you."

My pulse quickens, fear curling around my thoughts like a vine. My heart races again, each beat drumming out a warning as I stare at the note, the words sinking into my mind. There's no escaping the feeling that I'm trapped in a web spun from my own choices, and the person behind it all knows me far too well.

The note slips from my fingers, fluttering to the floor like a fallen leaf in autumn. I feel its weight pressing against my heart, a reminder that the past has a peculiar way of resurfacing when least expected. My pulse quickens, and I sink deeper into the couch, grappling with the creeping dread that wraps around me like a thick fog. The words are simple yet profound, each syllable echoing in my mind like a mantra I never asked to hear. "You can't escape your past. It will always find you."

I try to shake it off, dismiss the ominous vibe like I'd flick away an annoying fly. But as I glance around my cluttered living room, it dawns on me: I've spent so long trying to build a life free of the shadows that once clung to me, only to have them come crashing back in with this chilling message. The laughter and chatter of the radio seem distant now, and I feel as though I'm sitting in a void where sound fades, leaving only the weight of the note pressing on my chest.

The air around me thickens, turning my once-cozy apartment into a prison of memories. Each framed photo on the wall seems to mock me with moments I can no longer reach. My fingers trace the edge of the note, hesitant but unable to ignore the unsettling feeling that this isn't just a random threat. It's personal. I've stirred something I shouldn't have, and now it's knocking at my door.

"Great, just great," I mutter to myself, pushing my hair back with a shaky hand. The thrill of my daily life has dulled to a jagged edge, and the darkness that used to be a mere afterthought now looms large. Suddenly, the world outside my window feels impossibly vast and filled with potential threats.

With a deep breath, I toss the note onto the coffee table, alongside the pile of scripts. They lie there, silent witnesses to my turmoil. But as I sit up, determination flickering like a candle in the storm, I refuse to cower in the face of this unwelcome reminder. I reach for my phone, fingers trembling as I scroll through contacts, lingering on Ellie's name.

"Hey, I need you," I whisper into the night, the words barely escaping my lips. But just as I'm about to hit call, the shrill ring of my doorbell slices through the thick tension hanging in the air. My heart leaps into my throat.

Who could it be at this hour? I edge toward the door, peering through the peephole. I can see a figure standing there, their face obscured by the dim hallway light. An impulse surges through me—a mix of instinct and curiosity. I can't keep hiding. I won't.

I fling open the door, prepared to confront whatever waits on the other side.

"Hello?" It's a stranger, his expression unreadable under the dim light. He's tall, with a well-defined jaw and deep-set eyes that seem to scrutinize me, weighing my worth in a heartbeat. "I'm looking for someone," he says, his voice low and steady.

"Who?" I challenge, crossing my arms defensively. I can feel the adrenaline coursing through my veins, ready for a fight or flight. "You have the wrong apartment."

He shifts on his feet, glancing past me into the chaos of my living room, the remnants of my disarray laid bare. "No, I don't. I'm looking for you."

"What do you want?" My heart races, dread curling tightly around my stomach as I grip the doorframe.

"I know you've received a message." His tone is flat, but there's an urgency in his gaze that sends a shiver down my spine.

"What message?" I stammer, even as I know exactly what he means.

"The note."

A chill runs through me, and I step back, trying to close the door, but he slips his foot in just in time. "Wait," he says, raising his hands in a placating gesture. "I'm not here to hurt you. I'm trying to help."

I pause, weighing my options. This could be a trap, a classic misdirect in a thriller novel. Or it could be a lifeline thrown by someone who knows more than I do. "Help? From whom?"

"From someone who wants you to be safe. I'm not your enemy."

The strange mixture of sincerity and urgency in his voice makes me hesitate. I glance back into the room, my sanctuary turned battleground, and then back at him. He stands there, poised yet somehow unassuming, as if he's just stepped out of the pages of one of my stories.

"I have information," he adds, his voice dropping to a conspiratorial whisper. "Information that could change everything."

I take a step back, letting the door swing wider. "Come in," I say, my voice barely above a whisper. I can't believe I'm doing this, letting a stranger into my space, my life, but I'm desperate. My choices have dwindled to a singular thread, and the notion of unraveling this mystery tugs at my insides.

He steps inside, scanning the room with an intensity that sends a shiver down my spine. "You need to listen closely," he says, turning to face me, his eyes piercing. "There's a reason you're being watched. You're caught in something much bigger than you realize."

I cross my arms, frustration boiling beneath the surface. "What are you talking about? Who's watching me?"

"Someone from your past. Someone who knows everything about you."

My breath hitches, and I can feel the walls closing in, the air thickening with the weight of his words. "You're being cryptic. Just tell me."

He runs a hand through his hair, a nervous gesture that feels out of place against the gravity of our conversation. "They've been waiting for the right moment to strike. And that moment is now."

"What do you mean? Why? Why now?"

"Because you've stirred up old ghosts." He steps closer, urgency etched into his features. "You went public with your story again, and that has consequences."

The implications wrap around me, and I feel the ground beneath my feet shift. The show, the broadcasts—it was all supposed to be an opportunity to move forward, to reclaim my voice. I hadn't anticipated dragging old shadows into the light. "What do I do?"

His gaze sharpens, and he leans in closer. "You need to trust me. There's a safe place where you can regroup, figure out your next move. But you have to leave tonight."

"What?" The panic in my chest flares, and I shake my head. "You can't be serious. I can't just—"

"I know it's a lot to take in, but if you don't act fast, you'll be trapped in a web you can't escape."

The walls of my apartment suddenly feel claustrophobic, the comforting mess morphing into a labyrinth of uncertainty. "I need time," I say, my voice trembling.

"There's no time. You need to decide now."

Just as I open my mouth to protest, the faint sound of footsteps echoes outside my door. I freeze, dread pooling in my stomach like a rock. "What's that?" I whisper, my heart pounding in sync with the encroaching footsteps.

The stranger's eyes widen, a flicker of alarm passing over his face. "They're here. We need to go. Now."

Without a second thought, he grabs my hand, pulling me toward the back of the apartment as the pounding at the door begins. My pulse races, confusion and adrenaline mixing like a potent cocktail. The past has indeed caught up with me, and I can't shake the feeling that whatever awaits on the other side is just the beginning of a terrifying chapter I never asked to write.

Chapter 12: A Name Unspoken

I stood in my dimly lit living room, the soft glow of my lamp casting long shadows on the walls. The room was cluttered with remnants of my life—old textbooks stacked haphazardly on the coffee table, a half-finished puzzle still awaiting the final pieces, and a stack of unpaid bills that seemed to mock my current state of financial distress. As I cradled the phone in my hand, the weight of his last words echoed in my mind, reverberating like an unwelcome chorus.

"Remember." The single word lingered, heavy and oppressive, curling around my thoughts like a vine choking a blooming flower. I was no stranger to the art of forgetting; I had perfected it over the years, hiding memories beneath layers of self-preservation. But whatever this caller wanted me to recall was buried so deep that I felt a physical ache at the thought of digging it up.

The silence of the room pressed down on me, thick and suffocating. I had been trying to reclaim my life, piece by painstaking piece, but it felt like trying to assemble a puzzle with missing parts. My therapist insisted I confront my past, that I could only move forward if I acknowledged the fragments I wanted to discard. But the more I tried to reach into the recesses of my mind, the more elusive they became, like mist evaporating in the morning sun.

As I settled back against the couch, a soft sigh escaped my lips. I was caught between wanting to remember and fearing what I might uncover. I imagined the caller sitting somewhere, a smirk playing on his lips as he waited for me to crack. Was he reveling in my confusion? The thought sent a shiver down my spine.

My phone buzzed again, jolting me from my thoughts. I glanced at the screen, heart racing at the prospect of seeing his number again, but it was a message from Sarah instead. "Hey! You up for a movie marathon this weekend? I need a break from reality!"

I chuckled, feeling a warmth spread through me at the thought of my best friend. Sarah had a talent for grounding me, her effervescent energy often cutting through my spirals of anxiety. She was the sunshine to my overcast skies, a relentless force reminding me that life could still be fun.

I quickly replied, "Absolutely! Popcorn and cheesy rom-coms all weekend?"

"Only if we throw in a horror flick. Gotta balance the sweetness with some scares!"

"Fine, but only if I get to choose the rom-coms. Deal?"

"Deal! I'll bring the snacks. Just keep the phone off, okay? You need a break from that mystery caller."

I hesitated, the weight of her concern settling heavily on my chest. Part of me wanted to tell her everything, but I had a knack for downplaying the severity of my problems, crafting them into palatable bites that wouldn't cause too much worry. Instead, I replied with a simple thumbs-up emoji, stifling the unease creeping back into my thoughts.

As the days slipped by, the nights grew longer. The calls became a grotesque routine, a nightly specter haunting my thoughts. I tried to stave off the growing sense of dread by surrounding myself with noise: music blared through my speakers, TV shows played in the background, and yet, the moment the world quieted, his voice invaded my space.

"Remember."

Each time he spoke that word, it was like a jigsaw piece landing perfectly in place, yet the picture it formed was as elusive as smoke. I found myself digging through old journals, searching for clues in faded ink and forgotten thoughts. My fingers brushed against pages filled with mundane details, a calendar filled with plans that never panned out, and snippets of conversations that once held meaning but now felt like echoes of a different life.

One night, while scrolling through social media, I stumbled upon an old group photo from college. There we were: a motley crew of bright-eyed students, faces flushed with laughter and dreams too big for our small-town minds. I zeroed in on one face in particular, an unmistakable grin that sparked a flicker of recognition deep within. I felt an electric jolt, a rush of warmth that threatened to pull me under.

"Liam," I whispered, the name escaping my lips as if it had been waiting in the wings for its moment to shine. He had been a bright spot in my chaotic world, a friend whose presence often felt like sunlight breaking through a storm. But life had a way of complicating things, pushing people apart when they should have been together.

The realization hit me like a tidal wave. Was this the connection my caller wanted me to remember? I needed to find Liam, to dredge up whatever past lingered between us.

Fueled by newfound determination, I began to sift through old contacts on my phone, searching for his name. As the screen lit up with my past connections, my heart raced. What if Liam had moved on, completely forgotten about our friendship? What if he didn't want to be found?

My thumb hovered over the screen, hesitating before I pressed call. I could almost hear the echoes of our laughter mingling with the ghosts of unsaid words. Maybe this was what I needed—a bridge back to a time when life felt simpler.

I exhaled slowly, pressing the button, and felt a sense of liberation wash over me. Whatever happened next, I was ready to face it.

I felt the cool metal of the phone pressed tightly against my ear, still buzzing with the echoes of that ominous voice, as if it were a cursed object I couldn't bear to part with. The silence that followed his departure wrapped around me like a shroud, heavy and stifling, making my breath feel labored. With a deliberate motion, I set the phone down, resisting the urge to toss it across the room. I wasn't quite ready to part with my tether to the outside world, even if it was laced with anxiety.

The fluorescent light from the kitchen flickered, and the hum of the refrigerator became the only companion to my spiraling thoughts. I moved toward the window, pulling back the curtain to peer outside. The streetlights cast a warm glow on the pavement, illuminating a world that felt both familiar and foreign, as if it belonged to a different version of me—one who hadn't spiraled down this rabbit hole of dread and confusion.

"Remember." The word echoed in my mind, now a haunting refrain. What was it I was supposed to remember? My mind flitted through snapshots of my past—giggling with Sarah over ice cream, late-night study sessions filled with caffeine and whispered secrets, the heady exhilaration of college days where dreams felt like tangible treasures just within reach. But nothing seemed to align with the caller's insistence.

"Get a grip, Ellie," I muttered to myself, shaking my head as if I could physically dislodge the feeling of foreboding. I rummaged through my kitchen drawers, half-heartedly searching for the remnants of comfort food. A snack might dull the edges of my anxiety, or at least distract me. As I sifted through bags of chips and a half-empty box of cereal, my phone buzzed again, and my heart jumped into my throat.

This time, it was Sarah. "You sure you don't want to talk about this mystery guy?"

I leaned against the counter, my fingers tracing the chipped wood. "Not really. It's just a prank caller or something. Nothing to worry about."

"Except it sounds like he's really trying to get to you," she shot back, her tone light but edged with concern. "Do you want me to come over? I could bring my special popcorn seasoning."

I smiled despite the weight on my chest. "As tempting as that sounds, I think I need to figure this out myself. It's probably just a random coincidence. I'll call you later, okay?"

With a sigh, I hung up, wishing I could push away my concerns as easily as I had dismissed her offer. But there was something deeper brewing beneath the surface, an unsettling feeling that clawed at the edges of my mind.

The following days turned into an agonizing blur. The phone calls came at odd hours, always with the same cryptic request to "remember." It was as if my life had been hijacked by a ghost from the past, an echo of something I couldn't quite grasp. Each time I picked up the phone, my heart raced with a mixture of dread and anticipation. I knew I should feel empowered to confront the mystery, yet I found myself shying away from the truth, tiptoeing around the very memories that could set me free.

I spent hours poring over old photographs, scrutinizing every detail, hoping for a glimpse of recognition that might offer a lifeline. One evening, amidst the scattered remnants of my college years, I came across a faded photo of a bonfire party—a memory hazy with laughter and the smell of smoke mingling with the crisp autumn air. There, on the edge of the frame, stood Liam, his laugh like music that resonated deep within me. The way the firelight danced across his features reminded me of warmth I hadn't felt in ages.

"Hey, remember that time you nearly set your hair on fire?" a voice teased from behind me.

I spun around, startled to see Sarah leaning against the doorway, a knowing smile plastered across her face. "What? You didn't think I'd come over just because you told me not to, did you?"

I couldn't help but laugh, the tension within me easing just a fraction. "Well, it's good to know you have no respect for my personal boundaries."

"Boundaries are for people who have their lives together, Ellie," she quipped, sauntering into the room, her presence a whirlwind of energy that knocked the air out of my apprehension. "Besides, you look like you could use some company."

She plopped down beside me, eyeing the scattered photos. "So, what's this all about?"

"I'm trying to piece together this puzzle," I said, holding up the photo of Liam. "I think... I think he might be the key to everything."

Her brow furrowed as she examined the picture. "He was always a wild card. Do you really think he has anything to do with your caller?"

"I don't know, but something about the way he looked at me back then... it felt significant," I admitted, my heart racing at the thought. "What if I forgot something important? Something I need to confront?"

"Or maybe it's all just a big coincidence," she offered, her tone light, but I could see the worry lurking in her eyes.

Before I could respond, my phone buzzed again, and we both jumped. The room seemed to hold its breath as I glanced at the screen.

"Unknown Caller."

"Don't answer it!" Sarah exclaimed, her voice rising in urgency.

But curiosity clutched at me like a vice. With a breath steeling my resolve, I pressed the button. "Hello?"

"This is just the beginning, Ellie. You need to remember." The voice dripped with a malevolence that sent chills cascading down my spine.

I opened my mouth to speak, but the line went dead, the call cutting off as abruptly as it had started.

"Who the hell was that?" Sarah's eyes were wide, her earlier humor evaporating like morning mist.

"I don't know, but I think it's time I found out," I whispered, feeling a swell of determination rise within me. "I need to find Liam. I need to face whatever is buried in my past."

As I grabbed my coat, ready to step into the unknown, Sarah reached out, gripping my arm. "Be careful, Ellie. This is not just about memories anymore."

With a nod, I turned toward the door, my heart pounding with the thrill of uncertainty. The night was dark and full of shadows, but the call of the unknown was stronger than the pull of fear. Just as I reached for the doorknob, my phone buzzed again, vibrating ominously in my pocket. I paused, glancing back at Sarah, who was eyeing me with concern.

"Do you want to answer that?" she asked, her voice barely above a whisper.

"Yeah," I said, pulling out the phone.

But before I could check the screen, it lit up with a new message. My breath caught in my throat as I read the words:

"Meet me where it all began. Tonight."

I exchanged a glance with Sarah, and the weight of unspoken fear hung in the air between us.

Chapter 13: Unseen Threads

The weight of his words lingers in the air, a leaden shroud that wraps around me, suffocating yet electrifying. I sit in my cramped studio office, the soft hum of the fluorescent lights doing little to stave off the shadows creeping into the corners of my mind. Memories flit around me like dust motes in a shaft of sunlight, enticing yet elusive, whispering secrets I'm desperate to uncover. I find myself sifting through old yearbooks, their spines cracked from years of neglect, as if they, too, are haunted by the past. The faces of friends long faded into obscurity smile back at me, frozen in moments of laughter and mischief, each snapshot a window to a life I once lived, a life tethered to a boy named Ethan.

His laugh echoes in my mind, a melodic chime that dances on the edge of my thoughts, beckoning me to remember. How can I forget the way his eyes crinkled when he smiled, or how we would sit on the bleachers, legs dangling over the edge, spinning tales of our dreams while the sun dipped below the horizon? Yet, now, the memories come tinged with an unsettling urgency, as if the very act of remembering has summoned a ghost. I flip through the pages, fingers trembling, searching for a clue—a name, a hint, anything that might unravel the mystery woven into my current reality.

The nights grow longer, my search yielding nothing but a hollow ache in my chest. Old photos lie scattered across my desk, sepia-toned relics of friendships and heartbreaks. I can almost hear the whispers of my past selves, beckoning me to listen. Yet, in the depths of nostalgia, an undercurrent of dread weaves through my thoughts, pulling me under. My heart races with each ping of my phone, each email sliding into my inbox with an eerie silence, like a thief in the night. I check my screen, breath hitching in my throat as I see another unsigned message—a taunting echo of his voice, wrapping itself around my spine like a vice. They're always vague, always unsettling, leaving me more anxious than before.

"You know me, don't you?" The words drape over me, heavy and oppressive, and I can almost hear his breath, feel the chill of his presence slithering beneath my skin. I'm no longer sure where the threat ends and my paranoia begins. My coworkers, oblivious to my torment, chatter away in the background, their laughter piercing through my haze like a blade. I envy their carefree nature, the way they dance through life without a worry shadowing their every step. It's as if I've become a character in a horror film, trapped in a narrative that twists and turns with each passing day, the script written by someone unseen.

Then, one fateful evening, just as the sun melts into a pool of molten gold outside my window, I receive a package at the station. The delivery guy's bemused expression as he hands it over sends a ripple of unease down my spine. I hold the plain brown box in my hands, feeling its weight, a palpable reminder of the chaos swirling around me. I tear it open, my heart pounding in rhythm with the growing anxiety in my chest.

Inside lies a small, weathered notebook, its pages yellowed with age, the cover marred with scuff marks that speak of untold stories. My breath catches as I recognize it—the same notebook I lost years ago, back when Ethan and I were still a duo. My fingers graze over the cover, as if touching a ghost. I flip through the pages, heart racing, and as I do, the air grows thick with dread.

Scribbled in the margins are notes about me—intimate, personal details that feel like a violation of my very essence. Each line of scrawl is a chilling reminder of someone lurking in the shadows, someone who's been watching me for years, lurking just out of sight. My mind spirals, piecing together a fragmented puzzle that threatens to consume me. I can hardly breathe, every inhalation steeped in confusion and dread.

Who is this person? How do they know me so intimately, yet remain a stranger?

A soft laugh echoes from the hallway, breaking the tension like glass shattering in slow motion. My colleagues, oblivious to my descent into paranoia, joke about the latest ratings and office antics. Their laughter feels foreign to me, a stark contrast to the reality crashing down around my ears. "What's wrong?" a voice interrupts my thoughts, and I turn to see Jenna, her brow furrowed with concern, arms crossed over her chest. She's always been the voice of reason, my anchor in the tumultuous sea of my life.

"Nothing," I lie, forcing a smile that feels more like a grimace. The weight of the notebook sits heavy in my bag, a malignant presence that urges me to share but holds me back. "Just some... old memories."

Her eyes narrow slightly, piercing through my facade. "You know you can talk to me, right? We're in this together."

I nod, but the reassurance feels flimsy against the tempest brewing within. I've always been the strong one, the rock amidst the storm. But as the sun dips below the horizon, leaving the world cloaked in twilight, I can't shake the feeling that the storm is just beginning, and I'm standing right at its epicenter, waiting for the inevitable crash.

As night descends, I clutch the notebook, a lifeline to a past that is both familiar and foreign. I sit in my dimly lit office, shadows dancing on the walls like specters, the whispered notes beckoning me to unravel their mysteries. A shiver runs down my spine as I flip through the pages, each one a reminder of the unseen threads that weave through my life, binding me to a past I thought I had left behind.

The air grows thick with a tension that prickles against my skin, each page of the notebook heavy with secrets that refuse to stay buried. I flip through the faded paper, feeling the grain beneath my fingers, the musty scent wafting up like ghosts escaping from their tombs. My heart thunders in my chest, a frantic percussion against the stillness that envelops me. The scrawled notes become a sickly sweet poison, their intimacy both tantalizing and suffocating. Each line hints at familiarity, a twisted sense of belonging that sends chills racing down my spine. Who would do this? Who could possibly know so much about me?

I stand abruptly, my chair screeching against the wooden floor, echoing in the silent office like a call to arms. "Hey, Jenna!" I call, but my voice trembles, barely above a whisper. When she pops her head in, her expression is a mix of concern and curiosity, a puppy waiting for its owner to throw a stick.

"What's up? You look like you've seen a ghost."

I chuckle, though it feels more like a strangled laugh than anything genuine. "I might as well have. You ever feel like someone is watching you?" I hold the notebook up, and her brows knit together in confusion.

"Is that... the notebook you lost? What's written in it?"

"Personal stuff. Really personal," I admit, my breath hitching as I watch her flip through the pages. "And there are notes in it—notes that aren't mine."

Her eyes widen, and the teasing tone in her voice shifts to something more serious. "Notes? About what? About you?"

"About me. Things I've never told anyone. Things no one should know." The weight of my words hangs between us, heavy and foreboding. "It's like a diary, but... not mine."

Jenna glances around the empty office as if expecting to find the mysterious author lurking behind a potted plant. "You should go to the police."

I shake my head, fear twisting in my gut. "What would I even say? 'Excuse me, officer, I have a mysterious stranger creeping into my life via emails and old notebooks?' They'll think I'm losing it."

"Maybe you should talk to Ethan," she suggests, a hint of mischief creeping into her tone. "He'd know something about your past, wouldn't he?"

The mere mention of his name sends a wave of nostalgia crashing over me, each memory laced with a bittersweet ache. "I haven't spoken to him in years," I murmur, the weight of my silence settling around us like a fog. "Why would he want to get involved in this?"

"Because it's about you, and he might know something. Besides, he's still your ex. There's a chance he might be concerned."

"Concerned? Or curious?" I shoot back, half-joking but with an edge of truth. Jenna rolls her eyes, crossing her arms.

"Look, it's up to you. Just don't ignore this. If you're feeling threatened—"

"Threatened?" I laugh, the sound brittle and sharp. "What a charming word. But I'm fine, really. I'll just figure it out."

She steps back, folding her arms across her chest, her eyes narrowing. "You don't have to be brave about everything. You can lean on people sometimes, you know?"

"Right, and look where that got me," I mutter under my breath.

Jenna rolls her eyes, as if she can hear the internal dialogue I'm trying to keep at bay. "Whatever you decide, just be careful."

As she leaves, I find myself staring at the notebook again, the weight of it drawing me in, like a siren's call. It feels like a tether, dragging me back to a version of myself that I'd thought I had long since buried. I reach for my phone, heart racing at the thought of reaching out to Ethan. The last time we spoke, it had been an awkward exchange, filled with unfinished sentences and unspoken regrets. But maybe that's the very reason I need to do this.

I thumb through my contacts, hesitating just a moment before pressing dial. The phone rings, each chime resonating with the mounting tension in my chest. My mind races, conjuring a million scenarios, each one worse than the last. What if he doesn't remember me? What if he does? Just as the call is about to go to voicemail, he answers, his voice a jolt of electricity.

"Hello?"

"Ethan," I breathe, the name heavy with the past.

"Is this...?" He trails off, and I can hear the surprise in his voice, laced with the uncertainty of who I've become since we last spoke.

"Yeah, it's me. I need your help."

"Help? Wow, that's... new."

"Look, it's serious," I say, cutting through his joking tone. "I've been getting these messages, and there's a notebook that I think belongs to me, but it has... notes in it. About me. Things I've never shared with anyone."

"What do you mean, notes?" He sounds more curious now, a spark igniting in his voice.

"Details. Intimate ones. It's like someone's been keeping tabs on me."

There's a pause on the line, the kind that stretches out uncomfortably. "What do you want me to do?"

"I don't know," I admit, frustration bubbling beneath the surface. "Just... can we meet? I don't want to do this alone."

"Sure. Let's meet at that coffee shop we used to love. The one with the blue chairs?"

A wave of nostalgia crashes over me, warm and welcoming yet tinged with sadness. "Yeah. I remember."

"Okay, how about tomorrow at four?"

"Perfect."

"See you then, Ash," he says, and there's a softness in his tone that sends a shiver of uncertainty through me. The line clicks dead, leaving me alone with my thoughts and the creeping dread of what lies ahead.

The next day arrives cloaked in an overcast sky, clouds heavy with promise. I arrive early, the familiar smell of coffee wafting through the air, mingling with the warmth of baked goods. I take a seat at our old spot, the blue chair worn from years of familiarity. My hands tremble slightly as I cradle my coffee, the steam rising and curling in front of me like tendrils of past conversations and laughter.

THE WEIGHT OF SILENCE

When he arrives, my heart races—his presence feels like a relic of a time I thought I had outgrown. His hair is tousled, and there's a light in his eyes that feels achingly familiar.

"Ash," he greets, sliding into the seat opposite me. "You look... well."

"Thanks," I reply, though my voice comes out sharper than intended. "So, I have this notebook..."

Before I can explain, a shadow passes behind him, a figure moving too quickly, almost imperceptibly. I catch a glimpse of a face, a flash of recognition that sends my heart into a freefall. "Ethan, wait—"

But it's too late. The door swings shut, and in that moment, I realize I'm not the only one with secrets.

Chapter 14: Fragments of Yesterday

The name hangs in the air, electrifying the mundane quiet of my apartment. Dylan. I hadn't thought about him in years, and yet the mere mention of his name sends a shiver racing down my spine. I almost drop the notebook, my heart pounding in a strange rhythm, like it's trying to tap dance its way out of my chest. I clutch the worn cover tighter, feeling the familiar creases that I'd absentmindedly traced countless times before.

Dylan was not just a name to me; he was a ghost, a memory drenched in nostalgia and regret. Back when I was young and reckless, he had been the flame that ignited my spirit, only to burn me in the process. Our story was tangled with laughter and late-night drives, secrets whispered under the stars, and dreams that felt too big for our small town. It was the kind of summer romance you read about, the one that ended far too soon and left a bitter taste in your mouth, like too-sweet lemonade.

The entry in the notebook is brief, almost dismissive, yet the scrawled letters seem to leap off the page, pulling me deeper into the past. There's a mention of a café, a specific booth with peeling green paint and a view of the lake where we once spent lazy afternoons, pretending we would never have to grow up. I can see it vividly—the way the sunlight danced on the water's surface, making it shimmer like diamonds, and how we would sit for hours, talking about everything and nothing, our laughter echoing into the summer sky.

As I turn the page, I can't help but feel a pull, an irresistible urge to revisit that café, to unearth the remnants of a life that feels almost foreign now. There's something in the way the notebook speaks, laced with urgency, as if the universe is nudging me toward a revelation I never sought.

I toss the notebook onto the coffee table, but it refuses to be ignored. The soft thud seems to echo my internal conflict. Should I chase after memories that were better left buried? The very idea feels reckless, like holding a lit match to dry leaves. But isn't there an alluring thrill in danger? Isn't that what I once craved?

With a reluctant sigh, I slip on my worn sneakers and grab a light jacket. The crisp autumn air beckons, carrying with it the scent of fallen leaves and distant woodsmoke. I need to know if Dylan still haunts that booth, if the ghosts of our shared laughter still linger in the corners. The thought of it sends a twinge of excitement through me, like a shot of espresso coursing through my veins.

The walk to the café is punctuated by memories, each step echoing with fragments of laughter and heartache. The world around me shifts slightly, as if I'm moving between realities, the past blending with the present. When I finally arrive, the familiar sign swings gently in the breeze, its faded letters almost unreadable. The café is unchanged, a relic of our youth, and stepping inside feels like crossing a threshold into a sepia-toned photograph.

I spot the booth right away, its paint even more chipped than I remember. My heart flutters as I slide into the seat, half expecting to see Dylan across from me, that lazy grin and twinkling eyes that could melt even the iciest of hearts. The waitress, a cheerful woman with curly hair and a knowing smile, approaches with a notepad in hand.

"Long time, no see! The usual?" she asks, her voice like warm honey.

I nod, unable to find my voice. The atmosphere is saturated with the aroma of freshly brewed coffee and baked goods, the kind of scents that wrap around you like a comforting hug. The walls are adorned with photographs of patrons from years gone by, their stories frozen in time, each image a testament to laughter and love.

I sit back and let the nostalgia wash over me, the memories crashing like waves. And then, as if the universe had conspired to bring my past crashing into my present, the door swings open, and in walks Dylan.

My breath catches. He looks different, older, but somehow the same. The years have sculpted his features, giving him a rugged handsomeness that tugs at my heart. I watch as he glances around, a flicker of recognition crossing his face when his gaze lands on me.

"Is this seat taken?" he asks, his voice still holding that playful lilt that used to send shivers down my spine.

I shake my head, stunned into silence as he slides into the booth across from me. There's a beat of awkwardness, a chasm of unspoken words stretching between us. I can feel my cheeks heat, caught between the memories of what was and the weight of what could have been.

"Wow, it's been a while," he says, breaking the tension. "I thought I might find you here."

"Guess some things never change," I reply, the sarcasm slipping out before I can stop it. "Still holding onto the past, I see."

He chuckles softly, the sound rich and warm, and it strikes me how easy this feels, how effortlessly we slip back into our old rhythm, as if no time has passed at all. "I prefer to think of it as... nostalgia," he quips, a teasing glint in his eye. "After all, this place has character."

Our conversation flows like the coffee that arrives—warm, comforting, and surprisingly invigorating. We laugh about our shared experiences, the trivialities of life that once felt monumental. Yet, as the laughter fades, a deeper current simmers beneath the surface, pulling us toward the unfinished business of our past.

"Do you ever think about... us?" he asks, his tone shifting, becoming more serious.

I freeze, the question hanging in the air like a stubborn cloud. The answer dances on the tip of my tongue, but it's tangled in the webs of my heart. I nod slowly, not trusting my voice to speak the truth. "Sometimes. But it's complicated."

"Complicated can be good, you know," he replies, leaning forward, his gaze intense. "Sometimes it's the messy things that lead to the best stories."

And just like that, the weight of yesterday begins to lift, giving way to a future laden with possibility, the notebook's secrets now taking shape in the light of an unexpected reunion.

The tension in the air thickens as Dylan leans back, a half-smile playing on his lips, his eyes dancing with curiosity. The mention of "us" hangs between us like a delicate thread, barely tethered but too fragile to ignore. I take a sip of my coffee, letting the bitterness wash over my tongue, a temporary shield against the swarm of memories threatening to spill out.

"Complicated can be good, huh?" I echo, pretending to contemplate the implications of his words while my heart races. "Is that your way of saying we should dive into the wreckage of our past?"

"Only if you bring the life jackets," he retorts with a smirk, and I can't help but laugh, the sound a little too loud for the cozy café atmosphere. The familiar banter feels like a warm embrace, a welcome distraction from the spiraling thoughts in my mind.

As the conversation flows, I discover a new depth to Dylan, one shaped by time and experience. He speaks of travel, of hiking through mountains that touch the sky and tasting the kind of food that ignites passion. There's an infectious enthusiasm in his voice, a spark that reminds me of who he used to be. I find myself leaning in, captivated by his stories, but the underlying tension never fully dissipates.

"I never imagined you would end up here," he says, his expression shifting to something softer, almost vulnerable. "I thought you'd be off conquering the world or something equally grand."

"Yeah, well, turns out conquering the world wasn't as appealing as it sounded," I say, keeping my tone light even though the words feel heavy. "I've settled for being a ghost in my own life. Just the occasional apparition floating through."

His gaze narrows slightly, the teasing glimmer replaced by a more serious undertone. "You shouldn't be a ghost, you know. You're too vibrant for that. Too alive."

I swallow hard, feeling a rush of emotions surging. The compliment flutters through me, igniting old feelings that I thought were buried. But before I can respond, the café door swings open with a flourish, and a flurry of wind sweeps inside, bringing with it an unexpected visitor.

"Dylan! There you are!" A woman strides in, exuding confidence like a bright beam of sunlight slicing through the dimness. She's stunning—long, wavy hair framing her face, and an effortless style that suggests she's stepped right out of a magazine. My heart sinks as I realize she's looking directly at him.

"Savannah," Dylan replies, his tone shifting slightly as he straightens in his seat. I feel an invisible line tightening around my chest. "What are you doing here?"

"I thought we'd catch up, remember?" She glances at me with a curious smile, her gaze lingering a beat too long before turning back to Dylan. "I didn't expect to find you here with... company." The way she emphasizes "company" makes my stomach churn.

"Just old friends reconnecting," Dylan says, his voice casual but with an edge that suggests a hint of discomfort. "We were reminiscing about the past."

Savannah's smile is dazzling, but there's a sharpness in her eyes, as if she's dissecting the air between us, weighing it against whatever expectations she holds. "Ah, the past. Isn't it charming?"

I can feel the unspoken tension shift again, and my heart races for entirely different reasons. The air feels charged, like static before a storm. "So, you two know each other?" I manage, injecting a note of playful skepticism into my voice.

"Just a bit of history," Dylan says, and his expression darkens, shifting into something I can't quite read.

"Dylan and I go way back," Savannah chimes in, her voice like silk. "He was quite the charmer."

A familiar pang of jealousy washes over me, igniting the latent insecurities I thought I had long since buried. "Was I?" Dylan replies, a teasing lilt creeping back into his voice, but it feels strained, almost forced.

"You were, still are," Savannah retorts, her playful tone unyielding. "But don't worry, I'm not here to ruin your reunion."

"Right," I say, my voice sharper than intended, but the sarcasm is a thin veil over my discomfort. "I'm sure that was the last thing on your mind."

Dylan shoots me a quick look, a silent plea to keep things light, but my irritation bubbles under the surface, threatening to boil over. "So, what's the occasion, Savannah? A charity gala or some kind of networking event?" I can't help the edge in my voice as I feign casual interest.

"Oh, you know, the usual," she replies, a carefree smile gracing her lips. "Just business meetings and socializing with the right people."

I can't suppress the bitter taste forming in my mouth. She's every bit the confident woman who would never struggle with insecurities, and I suddenly feel like a mismatched puzzle piece in this picture-perfect world.

"Good to know you're still up to your old tricks," Dylan says, and the playful tone in his voice carries a weight of history. "I hope you're not pulling me back into that whirlwind."

She laughs lightly, a sound that's both beautiful and unsettling. "Please, you love a good adventure. I just came to remind you of what you're missing."

And just like that, the casual banter shifts again, morphing into something more complicated, and I can feel the threads of our reunion unraveling. My heart races as I lean back, desperately searching for a way to steer the conversation back to familiar shores, to the ease we once shared.

"What if we all shared a good adventure?" I say, the words tumbling out before I can fully process them. "You know, maybe a trip down memory lane."

Dylan raises an eyebrow, intrigued but wary. "And what does that entail?"

"Oh, just reliving those late-night escapades, perhaps?" I reply, forcing a smile. "Like that time you tried to jump the creek and landed in it instead."

A smile breaks across Dylan's face, a brief respite from the tension that envelops us. "I remember that. You were my only witness to the grand disaster."

Savannah chuckles, but there's something in her expression that tells me she's not as amused as she pretends to be. "What a delightful memory," she interjects, her voice light but the underlying tone dark. "But I think Dylan has moved on to bigger things."

"I'm still here," Dylan says firmly, his gaze darting between us, the unspoken questions in his eyes amplifying the atmosphere thick with uncertainty.

I sense an undeniable shift in the dynamic, a tug-of-war over memories that feel more like a battlefield than a trip down nostalgia. As we laugh and banter, I realize that the notebook has not only drawn me back into the past but has also tangled me into the present, binding me to a history I'm not sure I'm ready to face.

But then, amidst the laughter and tension, Dylan's phone buzzes on the table, a stark interruption. He glances at it, and I catch a glimpse of concern flickering across his face.

"I need to take this," he says, standing up abruptly, his voice low and serious.

I watch him walk away, a sudden chill filling the space he leaves behind. Savannah's gaze follows him, a sly smile creeping onto her lips as she leans closer, her voice dropping to a conspiratorial whisper. "You know, it's funny how the past has a way of catching up with us."

My heart races as I lean in, the tension thickening with every word. "What do you mean?"

Her eyes sparkle with mischief, a dangerous glint that sends a shiver down my spine. "Just that some secrets are best left buried. You never know what skeletons might be waiting to walk out of the closet."

The door swings shut behind Dylan, and as I sit there, the weight of her words hanging ominously in the air, I can't shake the feeling that I'm standing at the edge of something far deeper and darker than I ever imagined. The notebook may have unearthed fragments of yesterday, but now I'm left wondering just how many secrets still lurk beneath the surface, waiting for the perfect moment to reveal themselves.

Chapter 15: A Voice from the Past

Dylan. The name rolls off my tongue like a forgotten melody, its notes entwined with the ghosts of my past. Memories unfold before me, their edges softened by time yet still sharp enough to cut. I can picture us: two kids in a small town, navigating the tangled web of adolescence, our laughter echoing against the weathered walls of the local diner. The flickering neon sign above us buzzed like a wasp, a persistent reminder of the summer nights we spent talking about everything and nothing. I remember the way his eyes sparkled when he laughed, how they held a hint of mischief—just like his smile, which was always a heartbeat away from something deeper.

The air feels thicker as I linger in these recollections, the warmth of nostalgia tinged with unease. I force myself to think back to the last time I saw him, that evening when everything had changed. We had been at the old oak tree, the one where we carved our initials—D and J, forever entwined in a promise we never made. The sunset spilled colors across the sky, painting it with hues of pink and gold as the warmth of the day faded into cool dusk. Dylan had looked at me, something serious flickering in his eyes. "You know I'll always be here, right?" he had said, the sincerity of his tone contrasting sharply with the unspoken words that hung between us. I had nodded, but deep down, I had felt the weight of my decision pressing down on me, urging me to leave it all behind.

Now, years later, I'm back in this town—a ghost haunting familiar streets. My heart quickens at the thought of him, the uninvited guest lurking in the shadows of my mind. Who would have thought that after all this time, I'd still feel that same flutter, that old spark? A whisper of a feeling I thought I had buried alongside my past, buried deep in the ground where memories rot and decay. I shake my head, trying to dispel the thoughts that threaten to consume me, but they cling stubbornly like autumn leaves to a tree.

I remember the calls—the late-night conversations filled with the unfiltered honesty that only distance can provide. "You're going to regret it," he had warned, his voice a low rumble that sent shivers down my spine. I had brushed it off then, confident that leaving was the right choice, a step toward freedom. But now, standing on the precipice of uncertainty, the regret claws at me like a stray cat looking for attention. Why was he resurfacing now, after years of silence?

As I lean against the counter, the cool marble pressing against my palm, I can't help but wonder what Dylan has been up to all these years. Did he stay here, anchoring himself to the life we had dreamt of escaping? Or did he sail off into the horizon, chasing his own dreams? I can't decide which thought hurts more—him moving on or him still being stuck in the same old routine.

The bell above the door jingles, and my heart leaps into my throat. It's been almost a week since I received the latest note, the one that made me spiral into this whirlwind of memories. My stomach twists with anxiety as I turn to look. The moment our eyes meet, time freezes. Dylan stands there, a figure carved from memory, his familiar silhouette bringing back a flood of feelings I thought I had neatly tucked away.

His hair is darker than I remember, tousled in a way that looks effortlessly charming. I can see the traces of age on his face, subtle yet profound, like the first lines on a well-loved book that speak of experiences lived. The mischievous glimmer in his eyes remains, but now there's something deeper—an understanding borne of life's trials that adds weight to the lightness of his smile.

"Jenna," he says, voice low and rich, wrapping around my name like a warm embrace. It's not the high-pitched excitement of youth but rather a soothing balm, something steady that makes my heart ache in ways I didn't anticipate. "I didn't think I'd see you again."

I force myself to respond, though my mind races, seeking the right words to bridge the chasm of silence we've endured. "Neither did I," I admit, my voice trembling slightly. "What are you doing here?"

"Just... needed to take a walk down memory lane." His eyes dart away, betraying a hint of vulnerability that surprises me. "I figured if I ran into you, maybe we could talk."

"Talk?" The word feels loaded, a boulder rolling down a mountainside. "About what? The past? The way we left things?"

He takes a step closer, and the air shifts between us. "No, not just that. I wanted to see how you've been. It's been a while."

I swallow hard, feeling the weight of his gaze. The questions I've buried rise to the surface, ready to spill out like an old wound being reopened. What if this conversation leads us back to that day beneath the oak tree, where I chose the future over the familiar? What if we were never meant to be just friends? But instead of answering my questions, he shifts his weight, his hands tucked in his pockets, an awkwardness hanging in the air, charged with the potential for both healing and hurt.

"Life's been... complicated," I finally say, finding the courage to meet his gaze. "But I guess that's true for everyone."

He nods, an understanding passing between us that feels as fragile as the autumn leaves outside. "You don't have to explain. I just wanted to know you're okay."

"Okay?" I scoff, surprised by the edge of bitterness in my voice. "Okay doesn't begin to cover it, Dylan. I left to escape, to find something different. And now I'm back, standing in the wreckage of all my choices."

"I get that," he replies quietly, his eyes steady, anchoring me. "But maybe it's time to start anew, to face the ghosts together."

I feel the spark of hope flicker within me. What if this was the moment I needed, the one that could reshape everything? The past is heavy, but perhaps it doesn't have to anchor me down. Maybe, just maybe, this voice from the past could help me navigate the labyrinth of my own heart.

The pause stretches between us, thick with unspoken words, like a tightly wound spring ready to snap. Dylan shifts his weight, leaning against the doorframe, his posture both casual and vulnerable. "Look, Jenna, I know things ended... complicated between us," he begins, his voice a rich baritone that wraps around me like a familiar blanket. "But I've been thinking a lot about the choices we made. About the distance we created."

"You think I haven't?" I counter, unable to keep the sharpness from creeping into my tone. "Every day since I left, I've relived that moment beneath the oak tree—what I said, what I should've said. The idea that I could've chosen differently haunts me."

His brow furrows, and I can see the wheels turning in his mind, processing my admission. "You had your reasons. I get that," he says softly. "But I never stopped caring, you know?"

I swallow hard, the truth of his words mingling with the bittersweet taste of nostalgia. "Caring wasn't enough back then, was it?" I reply, my voice faltering. "We were kids playing with fire, and I ended up getting burned."

For a moment, his expression shifts, a flicker of regret crossing his features. "Maybe we were too young to know how to handle it," he offers, his gaze steady. "Or maybe we just didn't want to face the flames."

My heart races, the metaphor hanging heavy in the air between us. Flames. The thought ignites something deep within me, a flicker of desire to explore the heat of what we never had. I glance outside at the remnants of autumn, leaves swirling in a soft breeze, their vibrant colors mirroring the tumult of emotions inside me.

"I can't pretend it doesn't still sting," I say, my voice barely above a whisper. "You were always the one I wanted to confide in, and when I left... I lost that."

A moment passes, our silence wrapping around us like a cocoon. Then Dylan takes a step closer, the air electric with unacknowledged tension. "What if we stopped letting the past dictate us?" he suggests, his tone tentative yet bold. "What if we started fresh?"

The idea both excites and terrifies me, sending my thoughts spiraling. What would that even look like? Can two people with so much history really start anew? My mind races with possibilities, painting scenarios both hopeful and frightening. I take a breath, trying to steady my pounding heart. "And how do you propose we do that? Pretend the last decade never happened?"

"Maybe not pretend," he replies, a playful grin creeping onto his face. "But we could, I don't know, start with coffee? Talk like we used to, without the baggage?"

I chuckle softly, appreciating the lightness he brings into this heavy conversation. "You think I'll just dive into coffee with you like it's no big deal? What's next? A stroll down memory lane?"

He laughs, the sound warm and infectious. "Why not? I know a great little café that still makes the best blueberry muffins in town. You used to love them."

The mere mention of those muffins transports me back to countless mornings spent at that café, the sweet aroma of coffee mingling with the warmth of baked goods. I can almost taste the sugar dusting on my fingertips, the way they melted in my mouth, filling me with a sense of home. But nostalgia isn't enough to wash away the years of distance that loom between us.

"Okay, coffee," I say slowly, weighing the word as if it were a precious gem. "But it's just coffee. No expectations."

"Just coffee," he echoes, the promise shimmering in his eyes.

As we walk side by side down the familiar streets, the echoes of laughter from my past entwine with the present. The sun dips lower, casting long shadows across the pavement, and I can't help but feel that this is a turning point. A chance to peel back layers of hurt and uncertainty, one sip at a time.

The café looms ahead, its weathered sign swinging gently in the breeze. A rush of excitement tinged with apprehension floods through me. The last time I was here, everything felt so different. I'd sat alone in a corner booth, drowning my sorrows in coffee as I processed my decision to leave. It felt like a lifetime ago, yet the scars from that time still linger.

"Ready?" Dylan asks, pulling me from my thoughts.

"Ready as I'll ever be," I reply, a nervous laugh escaping my lips.

Inside, the café buzzes with life, a symphony of clinking mugs and soft chatter. The barista greets us with a smile, her warmth washing over me like a comforting hug. I scan the room, feeling the nostalgia wrap around me like an old sweater—familiar yet slightly uncomfortable.

We order our drinks, and as we find a small table in the corner, I catch sight of a couple sharing a slice of cake, their fingers brushing, laughter spilling like sunlight. I glance back at Dylan, who's watching me, a hint of mischief dancing in his eyes. "You remember the time we tried to share a slice of cake and ended up getting frosting all over our faces?"

"Please, that was more like a food fight," I retort, laughing at the memory. "I still can't believe I let you talk me into that."

He grins, the warmth of his smile a balm for my doubts. "You were always the one willing to take a risk. I admired that about you."

A heaviness settles back into my chest at the implication. "And yet I ended up running away from everything that mattered."

His expression softens, the lightness of our banter replaced by something deeper, more serious. "Sometimes running away feels like the only choice, but it doesn't mean we have to stay away forever."

I nod, contemplating his words. The coffee arrives, steaming mugs perched on the table, and as we take our first sips, the warmth seeps into my bones, grounding me. "So, what have you been up to all these years?" I ask, curiosity getting the better of me.

Dylan leans back in his chair, contemplating. "After you left, I stayed here, tried to make sense of it all. Took up photography—mostly landscapes at first. Then people. I realized capturing moments was a lot like remembering; it made things feel alive again."

"That's beautiful," I reply, genuinely moved. "I always knew you had an eye for detail. Your pictures must be incredible."

He shrugs, a modest smile playing at his lips. "Maybe one day I can show you. But enough about me—what about you? What's it like to chase your dreams? Did you find what you were looking for?"

The question hangs in the air, a fragile thread that could unravel with just a tug. I hesitate, unsure how much to reveal. "It's... complicated," I finally admit. "I chased a dream, but it turned out to be more of a mirage. I've had my highs and lows, but I'm still searching for that sense of belonging."

"I get it. It's like standing at the edge of the ocean, wanting to dive in but not quite ready to get wet," he offers, a playful glint in his eyes.

"Exactly! Sometimes I think I'm all set to leap, but then fear holds me back. It's exhausting."

His gaze intensifies, a flicker of understanding passing between us. "Then let's leap together, Jenna. What's stopping us?"

Before I can respond, the café door swings open, and a chill rushes in, pulling my attention. My heart drops as a figure enters, the light catching on the familiar features that feel like a thunderclap from the past. Ethan. My ex, the one I left behind, stands there, scanning the room. And just like that, the fragile moment between Dylan and me shatters, leaving me breathless with uncertainty.

Chapter 16: Confrontation

I can't live with the uncertainty any longer. Each day without answers gnaws at me like an uninvited guest, refusing to leave my thoughts. I track down Dylan, my long-lost friend, in a small town just outside Boston. The late afternoon sun casts long shadows on the quaint streets, where the air smells like fresh pastries and strong coffee, mingling with the crispness of the early fall breeze. It's a stark contrast to the turmoil brewing in my chest. When I see him for the first time in years, my stomach twists in knots—a reaction so visceral, it surprises me. He looks different—older, harder—but there's a glimmer in his eyes that brings a rush of nostalgia, reminding me of the boy I once knew, the one with a crooked smile and laughter that echoed in the halls of our shared past.

I step into the coffee shop, a cozy little place filled with the rich aroma of roasted beans and the soft murmur of conversation. It feels as if the world outside has faded away, leaving only the bittersweet weight of my memories. The warmth of the interior doesn't seep into my bones; instead, it amplifies the chill crawling along my spine. Dylan sits at a corner table, fingers wrapped around a chipped mug, his expression inscrutable. I take a breath, the air heavy with anticipation, and slide into the seat across from him.

"Hey," I manage, my voice barely rising above the din of the café.

"Hey," he replies, a hint of surprise in his tone. He looks me up and down, as if trying to reconcile the girl I was with the woman I've become. "You found me."

"Yeah, well, it's not like you were hiding," I quip, forcing a smile that feels more like a grimace. The tension crackles between us like static electricity, and I can't shake the feeling that we're both teetering on the edge of something precarious.

We start talking about mundane things—the weather, the coffee, the old high school teachers who somehow still seem to haunt the place. But as the conversation drags on, the air grows thick with unspoken truths, secrets coiling in the corners of his smirk. My heart beats loudly in my ears, drowning out the comforting sounds of espresso machines and soft chatter. I want to believe he's innocent, that he couldn't possibly be the one behind the calls that have terrorized my nights. But the longer we talk, the more I see something dark flicker in his gaze, a shadow that dances just beyond my reach.

"So, what have you been up to?" I ask, the question hanging like a fragile ornament, ready to shatter if pushed too hard.

He shrugs, an enigmatic gesture that speaks volumes. "You know how it is. Life, jobs, people. Nothing too exciting."

I press on, my instincts honed like a detective chasing down a lead. "Still in town?"

"Not really. Just visiting some old haunts." His words slide off his tongue, and I catch a glimpse of something sharper beneath the surface.

"Your old haunts? Like you're looking for ghosts?" I try to make light of it, but the way he stares at me, unblinking, sends a shiver down my spine.

"Something like that." He finally cracks a smile, but it's brittle, like it might splinter if poked. I can't tell if he's joking or if the weight of whatever he's carrying is pressing down on him like a lead blanket.

The conversation drifts, weaving through the familiar and the new, yet somehow it all feels like a game of charades, each of us carefully avoiding the words that would unravel everything. I find myself analyzing every word he says, every inflection in his voice. Is he being evasive, or is it my imagination? There's an undercurrent to his stories—veiled references to things only the caller would know, memories twisted into something dark and unrecognizable.

"You still work at the same place?" he asks, a flicker of interest sparking in his eyes.

"Yeah, still at the agency. It's busy, but I like it." I pause, gauging his reaction. "I've actually been getting these weird calls lately. Someone keeps... well, harassing me."

The smile vanishes from his face, replaced by a seriousness that unnerves me. "That sounds awful. Have you reported it?"

"Of course." My voice is steadier than I feel. "But they always slip through the cracks. It's like trying to catch smoke with your bare hands."

"People are strange," he says, the words dripping with an edge that makes my stomach churn. "You never really know what they want, do you?"

The glimmer in his eyes twists into something more sinister, and the realization hits me like ice water. I lean forward, daring myself to probe deeper. "Dylan, do you know anything about these calls?"

He leans back, a practiced motion that radiates casual indifference. "Me? No. Why would I?"

But the hesitation in his tone speaks louder than his denial. A knot of dread unfurls in my chest, a deep-seated knowledge settling over me like a shroud. I leave the coffee shop feeling more unsettled than ever, my heart racing as I replay every moment, every laugh that felt too light for the gravity of the situation. Dylan may not have said the words outright, but I know. I know he's the one.

The crisp air outside feels sharper than ever, each breath I take a reminder of the storm brewing within me. The gentle breeze ruffles my hair, but it can't cool the heat pooling in my chest. I step into the street, the café door swinging shut behind me with a muted thud, and take a moment to steady myself. The world around me continues with its mundane rhythm—people walk their dogs, children laugh, and the sun dips low, painting the sky in vibrant oranges and purples. Yet, all I can think about is the shadow that looms larger with each passing moment.

I wrap my arms around myself, not from the chill but from the gnawing realization that Dylan might be the very ghost haunting my life. I head toward my car, each step heavy with the weight of unspoken truths. Once inside, I slam the door as if I could shut out the chaos swirling in my mind. I grip the steering wheel tightly, my knuckles turning white as I fight to regain control.

Thoughts of Dylan tumble through my mind like a jumbled puzzle—pieces that don't quite fit together, but I know if I just stare long enough, the picture might become clearer. I replay our conversation, every laugh, every sideways glance. Was it paranoia or was there a real threat behind those charming smiles and casual comments? My phone buzzes in the cup holder, pulling me from my spiraling thoughts. I glance down to see a text from Sarah, my ever-optimistic friend.

"How did it go? You know I'm rooting for you!"

Her unwavering support is like a warm blanket on a cold night, but even her encouragement feels flimsy against the revelations swirling around me. I type back a quick response, "Not great. I need to figure some things out." The reply barely scratches the surface of the turmoil I'm feeling, but it's all I can muster at the moment.

With a sigh, I start the car and pull out of the parking lot, my mind racing as I try to connect the dots. The town begins to blur past me, and the deeper I delve into my thoughts, the more I realize that this confrontation is far from over. If Dylan is indeed involved in these unsettling calls, then I need more than just an explanation—I need proof. My heart races at the thought of confronting him again, but a quiet determination settles in. I refuse to be a victim of my own fear.

That night, the silence in my apartment is suffocating. The shadows stretch across the walls, whispering secrets that dance just beyond my reach. I pour myself a glass of wine, hoping it might soothe the clamor in my mind, but instead, it amplifies the echo of uncertainty. My phone buzzes again, a reminder that the world hasn't forgotten about me, even if I wish I could forget it for a while. It's a notification from the police department, a reminder that I still need to file a report about the harassment. I roll my eyes, setting the glass down hard enough to spill a little. The last thing I need is more bureaucracy to sift through.

My thoughts drift back to Dylan, to the fleeting moments of connection mingled with the heavy weight of suspicion. What happened to the boy who used to joke about his life being a sitcom? I can't reconcile that image with the man sitting across from me, cloaked in ambiguity. My resolve hardens. I need to dig deeper, to uncover whatever truth lies beneath the surface.

The next day, I decide to revisit the coffee shop, hoping for some kind of cosmic insight or perhaps a hint of clarity. The familiar aroma of coffee greets me as I push the door open, and for a fleeting moment, it feels like a normal day. I order a black coffee—strong, no sugar. Just like my resolve. As I sip it, I scan the room, searching for a sign, a clue, something that could connect the dots.

Then I spot him. Not Dylan, but a familiar face I hadn't expected. Sam, my old neighbor, is sitting at the table by the window, engrossed in a book. His presence sends a jolt of recognition through me, and for a moment, it distracts me from my racing thoughts. I hadn't seen him since he moved to a different part of the city, and he looks surprisingly well put together. I wave him over, desperate for a familiar voice amidst the chaos.

"Hey! Sam! Fancy seeing you here!" I say, forcing a brightness into my tone that feels slightly hollow.

He looks up, surprise lighting up his face. "Wow, it's been ages! How have you been?"

We exchange pleasantries, and I can't help but feel a twinge of relief in his company. But my mind is still tangled in the web of Dylan's deceit. "You wouldn't believe the kind of week I've had," I confess, leaning in slightly. "I think someone is messing with me."

"Messing with you how?" he asks, concern flashing in his eyes.

I glance around, half-expecting shadows to listen in. "I've been getting these calls, and they feel... personal. Like someone knows things about me that they shouldn't."

Sam's brow furrows, his expression shifting from casual curiosity to genuine worry. "That sounds intense. Have you talked to the police?"

I nod, but my thoughts drift back to Dylan. "I just feel like there's something more to it. Like someone is playing a game."

"Have you thought about digging into your past? You know, sometimes it's the people you least expect." His words hang in the air, and a chill runs down my spine.

"People like Dylan?" I can't help but blurt out, my heart racing.

"Wait, you saw him?" Sam's eyes widen. "I thought you two were done."

I shake my head, a mix of frustration and helplessness surging inside me. "I thought so too. But now..."

The air grows heavier as I share my encounter with Dylan, my words tumbling out in a rush, spilling my fears and suspicions onto the table like a spilled drink. As I talk, I notice a flicker of something in Sam's expression—an understanding, a concern.

"What if it's not just about the calls?" he suggests, his voice low and deliberate. "What if someone is trying to provoke you? Get you to react?"

The realization hits me like a punch. I have been so focused on figuring out Dylan's connection to the calls that I haven't considered the possibility that someone else is pulling the strings. My mind races through the scenarios—who would want to provoke me, and why?

Suddenly, my phone vibrates on the table, breaking through the haze of dread. I glance down to see a number I don't recognize flashing on the screen. My heart skips a beat, and for a moment, I consider ignoring it. But something compels me to answer. I press the phone to my ear, my heart pounding.

"Hello?"

THE WEIGHT OF SILENCE

Silence stretches on the other end, but then a voice, distorted and gravelly, cuts through the quiet. "You should have left it alone."

The world around me blurs, and the weight of the realization slams into me like a freight train. Before I can respond, the line goes dead, and I'm left holding my breath, caught in the web of uncertainty, adrenaline flooding my system. Sam watches me, eyes wide, and I know, without a doubt, that the game has just begun.

Chapter 17: A Twist in the Dark

The neon lights of the café flickered, casting playful shadows on the faded wooden tables, where the scent of freshly brewed coffee mingled with the sweet undertones of pastries that had seen better days. The air was thick with anticipation, a tangible buzz that thrummed against my skin as I clutched my phone, the screen still illuminating Ethan's frantic words: "You're in danger." It was all so absurd. How could I possibly be in danger? I was just a late-night radio host spinning tales to a scattered audience, crafting drama in the safety of my sound booth. Yet here I was, on the verge of unraveling a mystery that I had unwittingly stepped into, and it was wearing a face I recognized all too well.

Ethan had been my anchor in the turbulent waters of my newfound fame, a comforting presence who fed my creativity with just the right dose of sarcasm and sincerity. Our banter had danced along the edges of something deeper, a connection thick with unspoken possibilities. But the urgency in his voice now wrapped around me like a coil, tightening with each ring of the café's old-fashioned bell as customers drifted in and out, blissfully unaware of the storm brewing in my heart.

I hadn't seen him in months, not since that rainy night when we had shared our secrets under the flickering streetlight, a night that felt like the beginning of something significant. I missed his mischievous grin, the way his blue eyes sparkled with mischief, but more than that, I missed feeling grounded, as if I could touch something real amidst the chaos of my life. As I waited for him to arrive, the minutes felt like hours, and the café's chatter faded into a dull roar. I couldn't shake the feeling that something was terribly off, a dark thread woven into the fabric of my existence.

When he finally walked through the door, the air shifted. Ethan looked different—his usual swagger replaced with an urgency that rendered him almost unrecognizable. The tousled hair I adored was now disheveled, and his cheeks bore the shadows of sleepless nights.

He caught my gaze, and in that fleeting moment, the world around us fell away. The clattering of cups and laughter turned into a distant hum, leaving just the two of us in our bubble of unspoken tension.

"I thought you weren't going to come," he said, sliding into the chair across from me. His voice was low, a conspiratorial whisper that made my heart race.

"What could possibly be so dangerous? I mean, I'm just a girl with a radio show," I replied, attempting to inject levity into the situation, but the quiver in my voice betrayed me.

Ethan leaned in, his expression grave. "Dylan isn't who he says he is. He's been lying to you."

The name alone sent a chill racing down my spine. Dylan. He had been my safe harbor, the one who made the dark nights feel a little less suffocating with his charm and easy laughter. I shook my head, trying to dispel the fog of disbelief clouding my thoughts. "What do you mean? He's just... well, he's just Dylan."

"Exactly. Just Dylan," he shot back, his frustration palpable. "But he's not just any Dylan. He's been watching you, and I think he's got a plan."

A thousand questions bubbled up, but all I could manage was a weak, "Why?"

"Because you're his ticket," he explained, urgency sharpening his features. "He thinks you can help him get what he wants. He's playing you, and you need to get out before it's too late."

My mind raced, grappling with the implications of his words. The warmth of our banter had just turned cold, and the tension coiled tightly around my chest. "I don't understand. What could I possibly have that he wants?"

Ethan rubbed his temples, as if trying to stave off a headache. "Your show. Your audience. Your voice. He believes that if he can manipulate your platform, he can manipulate the narrative, control the story. And God knows what he's willing to do to get it."

I leaned back in my chair, my thoughts spiraling as I processed the weight of his revelation. My mind flickered back to our late-night conversations, the moments when Dylan had seemed too interested in my world, the way he had nodded enthusiastically at every crazy idea I pitched on-air. Had I been too naïve to see the signs?

"Why didn't you tell me this sooner?" I demanded, feeling the sting of betrayal prick my heart. "You were in the perfect position to warn me!"

"Because I didn't know!" he shot back, exasperation spilling over. "I thought you were happy. I thought he was just charming—"

"Charming?" I echoed, incredulity threading my voice. "You call this charming? I've been in the dark, and you let me play the fool while he's been plotting behind my back!"

"Because I didn't want to ruin it for you!" he said, exhaling sharply. "But I can't sit back and watch you put yourself in harm's way."

The café faded into the background, and in that moment, we were two people caught in a whirlwind of secrets and half-truths, each breath echoing with unspoken possibilities. I wanted to scream at him, to tear apart the carefully built walls that had kept my heart hidden, yet a part of me understood the turmoil within him, the desperation to protect me from a danger I could barely comprehend.

But my heart raced for a different reason now, the thrill of the chase igniting a fire within me. I had built my life on the stories I told, the twists and turns that captivated my audience. Maybe it was time to uncover the truth that lurked in the shadows.

"Then tell me how we get ahead of him," I said, steeling my resolve, my pulse quickening with newfound determination. "Let's turn the tables."

Ethan's brow furrowed, a flicker of admiration glinting in his eyes as he realized that the girl he knew was still there, beneath the weight of uncertainty. "Are you sure you want to do this?"

"Yes," I said, my voice steady. "But if we're going to face this, we need a plan. I won't let him have control over my life. Not anymore."

He nodded, and just like that, the air around us shifted again, crackling with a dangerous energy that promised a fight worth having.

With a plan tentatively forged between us, we dove headfirst into the murky waters of this conspiracy, armed only with our wits and a few stolen glances. The café became our headquarters, the chipped table a makeshift strategy board as we whispered ideas and concocted our next moves. Ethan's earlier agitation began to ebb, replaced by a focused intensity that made me both nervous and excited.

"I've been doing some digging," he said, pushing his hair back, revealing a small scar above his brow that I had never noticed before. "Dylan's past isn't as squeaky clean as he pretends. There are rumors—some pretty dark ones."

I frowned, the name now hanging like a weight in the air between us. "What kind of rumors?"

"Let's just say, he's had some run-ins that haven't exactly made headlines. People tend to disappear when they get too close."

A chill skittered down my spine, and I instinctively wrapped my arms around myself. "Disappearing? Like…gone without a trace?"

"More like dead or worse. It's not just about you anymore. He's got a pattern, and you might be his next target."

I opened my mouth to respond, but the words caught in my throat. A part of me wanted to dismiss his concerns as paranoia, but the other half—a darker, more instinctual part—recognized the truth behind his worry. "And you know this how?"

He leaned in closer, lowering his voice. "I have a contact who used to work with him. Said he was shady, manipulative, always wanting something from someone. We need to tread carefully. One wrong move, and we could find ourselves in deep trouble."

"Then we'll make the right moves." I squared my shoulders, determination hardening my resolve. "Let's go to his place and see what we can find."

"You're joking, right?" His eyes widened, disbelief etched on his features. "We can't just waltz into his den. He'll know we're onto him."

"We need to know what he's hiding. If he's been playing me, I want proof. And if I have to confront him, then so be it. It's time to face the music."

Ethan hesitated, the storm brewing behind his eyes, a mix of admiration and concern. "You're stubborn, you know that?"

"Stubbornness is my middle name," I shot back, a grin breaking through the tension. "Come on, let's grab our detective hats and go on a little adventure. I could use a break from the on-air drama."

He chuckled, shaking his head as he reluctantly agreed, the corners of his mouth lifting. "You're insane, but I suppose that's why I like you."

We slipped out of the café, the world outside bustling with life as if it had no idea the darkness we were about to plunge into. The streets were alive, lit by the soft glow of streetlamps flickering against the encroaching night. I could feel the adrenaline coursing through my veins, every pulse a reminder that I was not just an innocent bystander in this twisted game.

Dylan's apartment building loomed ahead, a tired structure that had seen better days, its brick façade marred by peeling paint and graffiti. "Let's keep it low-key," Ethan whispered, his voice laced with urgency. "If he's here, we don't want to alert him."

As we approached the entrance, I felt a peculiar sense of déjà vu, as if the very walls were closing in on me. The sound of my heart echoed in my ears, drowning out the chatter of the city. Ethan glanced around, ensuring the coast was clear, before pushing the door open and ushering me inside.

The hallway was dimly lit, and the scent of stale pizza wafted through the air, an uninvited reminder of the lives lived within these walls. We crept towards his apartment, my pulse quickening with every step. I could hardly breathe, the tension coiling tightly in my chest.

"Here we are," Ethan said, stopping in front of a door marked with a worn-out number. "Ready?"

"As I'll ever be," I replied, forcing a calmness I didn't feel.

Ethan hesitated for a moment, his hand hovering over the doorknob. "If he catches us, we might not get a chance to explain ourselves."

I nodded, steeling myself for whatever lay behind this door. "Then let's be quick."

With a swift twist, he turned the knob, pushing the door open just a crack. The room beyond was dark, the shadows pooling in the corners like secrets waiting to be uncovered. Ethan peered in, then motioned for me to follow. The air was thick, charged with the promise of discovery and danger.

Stepping inside, I felt a rush of exhilaration mixed with dread. The living room was a cluttered mess of mismatched furniture, an unmade bed shoved against the wall, and remnants of takeout strewn across the coffee table. But it was the small desk in the corner that drew my attention. Papers lay scattered, notes scrawled in a hurried hand.

"Look at this," I whispered, moving closer to the desk as Ethan followed. My fingers brushed against the papers, flipping them over one by one. "It looks like he's been keeping track of...something."

"Calls?" Ethan suggested, leaning in to read the hastily written notes. "He's tracking your show."

"What? That's insane." My mind reeled at the implications. "Why would he do that?"

"Maybe to gauge your influence. To see how many people are listening, who they are. If he's planning something, he needs to know the lay of the land."

Before I could respond, a noise echoed from the back of the apartment—soft, cautious footsteps. My heart dropped, and I shot Ethan a panicked glance. "Someone's here."

"Hide!" he hissed, and we both dove behind the couch, the fabric scratching against my skin as I tried to stifle my breathing.

I could hear the footsteps growing louder, the sound echoing like a thunderclap in the silence. The tension was thick, and I held my breath, praying that whoever had entered would remain oblivious to our presence. The door creaked open, and a figure stepped inside, silhouetted against the dim light spilling in from the hallway.

"Dylan," I breathed, recognizing him immediately.

But something was off. His expression was tense, his brow furrowed, and as he stepped further into the room, I caught sight of what he was clutching—a small, ominous-looking briefcase. My heart raced as he moved towards the desk, his eyes scanning the chaos, searching for something.

"Where is it?" he muttered to himself, a mixture of frustration and fear tinging his voice. "I know it was here."

I exchanged a worried glance with Ethan, his eyes wide with disbelief. What could be in that briefcase? And why was Dylan so anxious?

"I have to get out of here," I whispered, my pulse quickening as I felt the walls closing in.

But before I could make a move, Dylan's head snapped up, his eyes darting towards the couch where we were hiding. "I know you're here," he called, his voice suddenly cold and sharp, slicing through the tension like a knife.

My heart plummeted, and I froze, dread coiling in my stomach.

"Show yourself!" he demanded, a predatory glint in his eyes that sent chills racing down my spine.

Ethan and I exchanged a panicked look, the realization hitting us like a freight train: We were no longer the hunters in this game. We had just become the hunted.

Chapter 18: Web of Lies

The lake stretches before us, a shimmering expanse of blue tinged with the gold of a fading sun, casting long shadows that dance across the surface. I had forgotten how beautiful it could be, this spot where laughter had once floated through the air like a gentle breeze, now replaced by the suffocating weight of unresolved emotions. Ethan's presence pulls me from my reverie, and the air crackles between us, heavy with everything we've left unsaid.

He shifts uncomfortably on the weathered wooden bench, his fingers tapping a nervous rhythm against his knee. I take a moment to study him, searching for the familiar features I once adored. The tousled hair that used to fall just above his eyebrows is now tinged with a hint of silver, his jawline more pronounced, bearing the weight of the years since our lives diverged. There's a weariness in his eyes that wasn't there before, a depth that speaks of burdens carried in silence. I can't help but wonder what kind of hell he's been through since we said our goodbyes.

"I thought you'd never come back," he finally says, his voice a gravelly whisper, as if he's afraid to disturb the tranquil surface of the lake.

"And I thought I'd never want to," I reply, my tone sharper than intended. I can feel my heart racing as I recall the years we spent together, the warmth of his touch, the comfort of his laughter. But that was before the lies, before everything fell apart.

He nods, almost as if he expected my response. "I know. But you need to hear me out. This isn't just about us anymore. It's about Dylan."

At the mention of his name, a chill runs through me. Dylan, the ghost of our past, always lurking in the shadows, waiting to strike. My pulse quickens as memories flood back—Dylan's charming smile, the way he could light up a room, and the insidious way he wove himself into our lives, creating fractures I never understood until it was too late. "What about him?"

Ethan takes a deep breath, his eyes flickering to the water. "He's been obsessed with you for years. Even when we were together, he was always there, whispering doubts into my ear, planting seeds of mistrust. I thought he was my friend, but he was the one pulling the strings, manipulating everything between us."

I shake my head, trying to process his words. "Are you serious? You really think he did all that?"

"I know he did," Ethan replies, his voice steady now. "I was blind to it, caught up in the whirlwind of my own insecurities. He made me believe that you were unfaithful, that you were looking for a way out, and it twisted everything. I thought I was protecting myself, but really, I just pushed you away."

My heart aches at the rawness of his admission, the vulnerability in his eyes. It's a strange sensation, this mix of anger and empathy. I want to scream at him for letting Dylan come between us, for letting the shadows of our relationship fester until they became a gaping wound. But I also see the hurt in his expression, the remorse clawing at him like a wild animal.

"So, what? Dylan's back to finish what he started?" I ask, my voice wavering slightly. "What does he want from me now?"

Ethan runs a hand through his hair, frustration etched into his features. "I don't know. But he's been showing up everywhere, and I've heard things. He's obsessed with you, and it's dangerous. I'm worried he's trying to manipulate you again, just like before."

A knot forms in my stomach, twisting tighter as I consider the implications of his words. "What do you want me to do? Just run away? Hide?"

"No." Ethan leans closer, urgency flaring in his gaze. "I want you to stand your ground. We can't let him take control of our lives again. We need to figure this out together."

I can't help but chuckle bitterly, the sound echoing off the water. "Together? After everything? You think we can just sweep the past under the rug and pretend it doesn't exist?"

"Maybe not sweep it under the rug," he counters, a glimmer of a smile breaking through his tension. "More like... put it in a box, tie it up with a bow, and lock it away in the attic. You know, a metaphorical attic."

His attempt at humor catches me off guard, and I can't help but smile, despite the storm brewing inside me. "A metaphorical attic? How charmingly domestic. What's next, a family scrapbook?"

"Only if you promise to include our pictures," he says, a playful twinkle lighting his eyes. "Before the chaos, of course."

The moment is fleeting, but it's enough to remind me of the warmth we once shared, the laughter that used to come so easily between us. But the weight of our past hangs heavily in the air, demanding acknowledgment. "This isn't a joke, Ethan. Dylan isn't just some ex-friend who had a grudge. He's dangerous. What if he decides to come after you next?"

Ethan's expression shifts, seriousness washing over his features. "Then we face him together. I refuse to let him control our lives anymore. We need to be smarter than he is. We need a plan."

"Easier said than done." I lean back, staring out at the lake, its surface reflecting the fiery colors of sunset. "What if he's already two steps ahead?"

A silence falls between us, charged with unspoken fears and the weight of past decisions. In that moment, I see the flicker of determination in Ethan's eyes—a spark of the boy I fell in love with, a reminder that maybe we could navigate this storm together. But the question remains: can we truly confront the ghosts of our past while facing the very real threat that lurks in the shadows?

The sun sinks lower, casting a warm golden hue across the water, and I'm reminded of how time can feel both infinite and cruelly fleeting. The way it trickles past us is akin to the water flowing over the stones beneath—a relentless push, unyielding, and just as unpredictable.

Ethan breaks the silence first, leaning in with an intensity that momentarily disarms me. "Listen, we need to be cautious. I didn't come here just to rehash old wounds. I need you to understand the seriousness of the situation. Dylan is not just some petty ex; he's dangerous. And he thrives on chaos."

The weight of his words hangs in the air, heavy enough to sink a ship. My heart races as the implications settle in my mind like sediment at the bottom of the lake. "What does he want, Ethan? Why now?"

Ethan sighs, a cloud of frustration passing over his features. "Power. Control. He sees your life, your success, and he wants to take it away. He thrives on the idea that he can manipulate people. It's his art form."

"Art form?" I scoff, incredulous. "Is that what we're calling it now? That's a generous label for someone who thrives on other people's misery."

He chuckles, but there's a somber edge to his laughter. "I'd call it a twisted form of creativity. He's always been good at weaving stories, making people see things that aren't really there. I let him get in my head. I let him pull me away from you."

"I still can't believe you would let someone like him get to you," I say, my voice low, almost shaking. "You always seemed so strong, so sure of yourself."

Ethan shrugs, the gesture half-hearted. "Even the strongest can break. I didn't know how to handle it. And honestly? I thought I was saving myself from a future heartache, but instead, I pushed you into his arms."

My breath hitches, the mention of Dylan igniting old flames of resentment. "You have no idea how much he messed with my head after you two turned me into a villain in your story. I was the bad guy, the one who didn't care about our relationship. And for what? Because of your insecurities?"

"I know," he replies, voice barely above a whisper, as though confessing a sin. "And I'm sorry. I was a fool. But now that I've figured this out, I can't let him manipulate you again. We need a plan. We need to outsmart him."

"Great. So we're going to play a game of chess with a guy who's already turned the board upside down?" I ask, sarcasm slipping into my tone. "How do we even know what moves he's going to make?"

"We keep our cards close to our chests. We don't give him any leverage." He leans closer, and I can smell the faint trace of cologne mixed with the earthy scent of the lake. It's grounding, almost familiar. "But first, you need to be aware of how he operates."

"Yeah, I think I have a pretty good idea," I retort, crossing my arms as I stare at the gentle ripples on the lake's surface. "You should've seen how he toyed with my emotions. I was just a pawn in his twisted game."

Ethan's gaze softens. "I didn't know. But I'm here now, and I'm not going anywhere. We'll expose him. If we can gather evidence—anything that shows how he's been pulling the strings—we can finally end this."

I consider his words, the prospect of standing up to Dylan stirring something fierce within me. The fire that once felt extinguished begins to spark again. "Okay. But where do we start?"

Ethan grins, a glimmer of the boy I once knew surfacing in his expression. "We start by investigating. I have a contact who might know where Dylan has been hanging out lately. I can set up a meeting, and we'll find out what he's up to."

"Great, but what if he finds out we're onto him?" My unease bubbles back to the surface, the familiar fear mingling with a strange thrill.

"He won't. Not if we're careful." Ethan's voice has a reassuring cadence, pulling me back from the edge of doubt. "We need to stick together. If we've learned anything from our past, it's that isolation only gives him power."

A shiver of resolve courses through me. "Together, then. Let's do this."

Just as we find our footing in this fragile alliance, a rustling sound echoes from behind the trees lining the lake. The tension thickens, as if the air itself is warning us. I glance over my shoulder, a creeping dread washing over me.

"What was that?" I ask, my heart pounding in my chest.

Ethan's eyes narrow, scanning the foliage. "I don't know. Stay close."

The rustling grows louder, a cacophony of breaking twigs and snapping branches, and suddenly, a figure emerges from the shadows. It's him—Dylan.

His familiar smirk is plastered across his face, a predatory gleam in his eyes that sends a chill racing down my spine. "Well, well, if it isn't the two lovebirds. I thought you'd be a little smarter than to meet here. But then again, I guess old habits die hard."

I exchange a glance with Ethan, the moment stretching taut between us. A hundred thoughts whirl in my mind—each one more frantic than the last.

"Dylan," Ethan says, voice low but steady. "What are you doing here?"

"Oh, just enjoying the view." Dylan's gaze flits between us, mocking and probing. "You're quite the sight, really. A reunion by the lake—how nostalgic. It brings back memories, doesn't it? Such a shame they're tainted with betrayal."

Betrayal hangs in the air like a thick fog, and I can feel it tightening around us, squeezing the breath from my lungs. "Get out of here, Dylan. You don't belong here," I say, trying to sound more confident than I feel.

He laughs, a cruel sound that echoes across the water. "But I think I do. You see, I'm not the one who's going anywhere. You are, and I'll make sure of it."

The world tilts, and in that moment, I realize the game has just begun.

Chapter 19: The Truth Beneath

A wave of uncertainty washed over me, drenching my resolve in icy dread as I stared into the depths of my coffee cup, its dark liquid swirling like the chaos inside my mind. The small café was a haven of comfort, filled with the aroma of freshly brewed coffee and the muted chatter of patrons seeking refuge from the outside world. Yet, even here, within these familiar walls, I felt like an interloper, an alien amidst the warmth and camaraderie. The barista, a woman with a shock of pink hair and an easy smile, floated around the room, her laughter punctuating the air. I envied her effortless cheer, the way she seemed to fit seamlessly into her surroundings. Meanwhile, I was trapped in a web of deception, unable to find my way out.

Ethan sat across from me, his fingers nervously tapping on the table, an unconscious rhythm echoing the anxiety thrumming beneath my skin. I caught his eye, and for a fleeting moment, I saw something unguarded in his gaze—an invitation to remember the days when trust was as natural as breathing. But those days felt light-years away now, eclipsed by the dark shadow of Dylan's manipulation. "You need to tell me everything," I urged, my voice barely above a whisper, the weight of my fear heavy on my chest.

"I wish I could," Ethan replied, his brow furrowing. "But I can't decipher Dylan's next move either. It's like he's playing a game with pieces only he can see."

Frustration bubbled within me, a hot tide rising up, threatening to overflow. "A game? This isn't a game, Ethan! This is my life!" The words slipped out sharper than I intended, slicing through the café's gentle hum. I quickly lowered my voice, feeling the weight of curious eyes upon us, whispering that I was the crazed woman whose life had become a twisted plot worthy of the worst kind of drama.

Ethan leaned closer, his expression earnest. "I know it feels like you're caught in a storm with no end in sight, but you have to remember, you're not alone. You have me."

His sincerity sent a shiver down my spine, but it wasn't enough to dispel the growing dread that gnawed at my insides. "What if this storm is just the beginning? What if Dylan has something planned that we can't even begin to fathom?"

Ethan's eyes darkened, shadows flickering over his features like a curtain drawing tight. "We'll figure it out together," he said, his voice steady, but I detected the flicker of uncertainty that mirrored my own. "We can't let him dictate how we live our lives."

I drew a breath, feeling the heat of his words wrap around me like a cocoon. Maybe I could allow myself to trust him, if only for a moment, to let down the barriers I had built so carefully. The thought was tantalizing, a sweet relief amidst the chaos. But just as quickly, a wave of guilt washed over me. "What about everything that's happened between us? How can I just forget?"

He leaned back, a flicker of pain crossing his features. "You don't have to forget. Just... remember what we used to be. Before everything turned upside down."

Those words hung between us, heavy and electrifying, and for the briefest moment, the world around us faded into insignificance. My heart raced, caught in a tumult of longing and resentment, the memories of stolen kisses and laughter echoing in the recesses of my mind.

But as quickly as it came, the moment shattered like glass against the floor, splintering into a million sharp, painful shards. Dylan loomed in the background, a dark specter that hovered just out of reach. I could feel him, a sinister presence creeping along the edges of my consciousness, relentless and unyielding.

"Why hasn't he made his move?" I murmured, more to myself than to Ethan. The question danced on my tongue, a haunting melody that refused to fade. "What's he waiting for?"

Ethan shifted, his expression growing serious. "Maybe he's trying to gauge your reaction, or he thinks he can toy with you until you break. That's the kind of sick game he plays."

My stomach churned at the thought, bile rising as memories of Dylan's twisted smile flooded my mind. I could still hear his voice, soft and soothing, promising me the world while hiding daggers behind his back. "But why let me twist in the wind?" I demanded, my frustration resurfacing. "If he's so sure of himself, why not just come after me?"

"I wish I knew," Ethan replied, his brow furrowed with concentration. "But maybe it's about control for him. Maybe he gets off on watching you squirm."

A chill crept up my spine, and I shivered, wrapping my arms around myself as though I could shield my heart from the frigid reality. "Control. That's always been his game." I pressed my palms against the table, feeling the cool wood beneath my fingers, grounding me as my mind raced.

And then, a thought struck me, sharp and clear. "What if he's waiting for me to make a mistake? What if he wants me to slip up?"

Ethan's gaze sharpened, and I could see the gears turning behind his eyes. "Then we can't give him that satisfaction. We need to stay one step ahead."

The urgency of his words ignited something within me, a flicker of determination that burned brightly in the darkness. This wasn't over; I could feel it in my bones. The stakes were higher than ever, and the game was about to escalate.

"Let's put our heads together," I said, a surge of resolve sweeping over me. "We need to outsmart him. He thinks he's the puppet master, but he's underestimating us."

Ethan nodded, the ghost of a smile creeping onto his lips, a spark igniting in his eyes that made my heart race. "That's the spirit. Let's show him just how wrong he is."

As we leaned closer, the noise of the café faded into the background, and for the first time in what felt like ages, I dared to hope.

The adrenaline coursed through my veins like wildfire, igniting a mix of fear and determination. I leaned in closer to Ethan, and our heads nearly touched over the table, a conspiratorial intimacy weaving between us. The clatter of cups and the soft hum of conversation faded into a distant echo, and all I could hear was the steady pulse of my heart, reminding me that I was still alive, still fighting.

"Okay," I began, my voice a murmur, tinged with the urgency that felt electric in the air. "If Dylan is waiting for me to slip up, then we need to be careful. We can't let him think we're panicking. He needs to believe he's in control."

Ethan nodded, his expression shifting from uncertainty to fierce resolve. "Exactly. We play it cool, like nothing's wrong. But we also need to dig deeper. He must have a weakness we can exploit."

I straightened, the weight of his words settling in. "A weakness... like a chink in his armor. What if he's not as untouchable as he pretends to be?" My mind raced, spiraling through the myriad ways Dylan might be vulnerable, the layers of his facade.

Ethan leaned back, tapping his fingers against the table as though composing a mental checklist. "Think about it. He's been playing this mind game for a while now. There has to be something—someone—who can rattle him. Maybe we can track down a connection or find someone he's crossed."

The idea blossomed in my mind, a fragile flower pushing through the cracks of concrete. "What about his friends? Or the people he's worked with?" I mused aloud, envisioning a network of potential allies, people who might be willing to share their experiences with the monster behind the curtain.

Ethan grinned, the lightness of the moment catching me off guard. "You've got it. If we can find someone who's seen behind his mask, that could change everything."

With newfound energy, I pulled out my phone and started scrolling through my contacts. "There's Mia. She was in his circle for a while. Maybe she knows something."

"Do you trust her?" Ethan asked, his tone turning serious again.

"Trust? It's a complicated word." I tapped my fingers against the screen, the vibrant café fading into the background as I dialed Mia's number. "But right now, I need information, and she might have it."

The phone rang, each beep echoing in my chest like a ticking clock, a countdown to something monumental. On the third ring, she picked up, her voice cheerful and a tad too bright. "Hey there! What's up?"

"Mia, it's me." My heart raced as I plunged into the conversation, the urgency thickening the air. "I need to ask you about Dylan. I know you've worked with him. Can we talk?"

A pause stretched between us, heavy with uncertainty. "Dylan? Is everything okay? You sound... intense."

"It's complicated. I just need to know if he's ever shown a different side, or if there's anyone who can tell me about him."

"Wow, that's a loaded question." Her voice turned cautious, the cheer evaporating like mist in the sun. "He was charming, but there was something off about him. I never really felt comfortable. There were rumors, though—things I never saw directly."

"Rumors? What kind?" My pulse quickened, the possibility of a breakthrough dancing just out of reach.

"There was this girl," she said slowly, weighing her words like fragile glass. "She worked with him and ended up leaving abruptly. I heard she was scared, but I never knew why."

"Do you know her name? Where I can find her?"

"I think her name was Clara. I don't have her contact info anymore, but I can reach out to some old colleagues."

"Please do. Every detail could help."

"Sure, I'll text you if I find anything," Mia replied, her voice firm, as if trying to reassure herself as much as me.

I hung up, a mix of exhilaration and anxiety swirling in my stomach. "She might have something. If we can find Clara, we could get closer to understanding what makes Dylan tick."

Ethan's eyes sparkled with enthusiasm. "We've got a lead. Now we need to capitalize on it."

Just as I was about to reply, the café door swung open with a gust of wind that brought a chill with it, causing the bell above to jingle sharply. My gaze snapped toward the entrance, and my heart plummeted as I spotted a familiar silhouette. Dylan stood there, a figure carved from shadows, his expression inscrutable as he surveyed the room, his eyes narrowing in our direction.

"Damn it," I breathed, the reality of the moment slamming into me like a freight train.

Ethan's hand shot out, gripping my wrist. "Stay calm," he hissed, his voice barely above a whisper. "He doesn't know we're onto him."

But as Dylan's gaze locked onto mine, I could feel the tension spike, thickening the air between us. I instinctively leaned back, the instinct to hide clashing with the urge to confront him head-on.

He stepped further into the café, confidence radiating from him like an electric charge. "Well, well," he said, his voice smooth and oily, dripping with that familiar charm that always managed to crawl beneath my skin. "What's this? A little rendezvous I wasn't invited to?"

Ethan's grip on my wrist tightened, a protective instinct surfacing that sent warmth coursing through me. "What do you want, Dylan?" I shot back, forcing myself to hold my ground, the heat of defiance igniting a spark within.

"Oh, just checking in on you both. I couldn't help but notice you two looking rather... conspiratorial." His gaze flicked between us, a predatory glint in his eye that made my skin crawl.

"Just enjoying coffee. It's a free country," I replied, attempting nonchalance but feeling the tremor in my voice betray me.

"Is that so?" His smile turned smug, a predatory gleam flickering beneath the surface. "I hope you're not planning anything without me. That would be quite rude, wouldn't it?"

A thousand thoughts raced through my mind, each one spiraling into a tangled web of possibilities. His words hung in the air, heavy with threat and manipulation.

"Are you threatening us?" Ethan challenged, his tone unwavering, a fierce protectiveness radiating from him.

Dylan laughed, a chilling sound that sent a shiver down my spine. "Threatening? No, darling, I'm merely reminding you of your place."

The walls felt like they were closing in, a claustrophobic pressure building as I locked eyes with Ethan. We were cornered, but I refused to back down. "You don't scare me," I shot back, the fire in my words igniting the tension crackling between us.

Dylan leaned in, a sly smile dancing across his lips. "Ah, but that's where you're wrong. You should be scared. The truth is coming, and it won't be pretty."

Before I could respond, he turned on his heel and strolled away, leaving behind a trail of ice that clung to my skin. My breath quickened as I absorbed the weight of his words, each syllable echoing ominously in my mind.

"Did he really just say that?" Ethan whispered, his brows knitted together in disbelief.

I shook my head, anger mingling with fear as I felt the ground shift beneath me. "He knows something. We need to act fast before he makes his next move."

Ethan's determination matched my own as we both realized we were on a precipice, the world around us holding its breath, waiting for the next wave to crash.

But just as the realization settled in, my phone buzzed violently against the table, a stark reminder that the game had only just begun. I glanced down at the screen, my heart stalling as I saw Mia's name flashing ominously.

"Don't leave me hanging," I muttered under my breath, the air thickening with tension as I picked up the phone.

Chapter 20: Through the Cracks

The clock on my nightstand blinks an accusing red, each tick echoing the rapid beats of my heart. I squeeze my eyes shut, hoping to block out the relentless thoughts swirling like autumn leaves caught in a gust of wind. Memories of Dylan crowd my mind, slipping through the cracks of my reality, each one laced with a sense of betrayal. I can almost feel the weight of his words, heavy and suffocating, pressing down on my chest. What did he want from me? Was I merely a pawn in a game I never consented to play?

The night stretches endlessly, and I can no longer ignore the dark undercurrents swirling in my life. I flip onto my back and stare at the ceiling, where shadows play tricks on my mind. The old paint seems to whisper secrets, a haunting lullaby that tugs at my consciousness. I can't shake the feeling that I'm missing something vital, a key that could unlock the tangled mess Dylan left behind.

With a restless sigh, I swing my legs over the edge of the bed, feeling the cool hardwood floor against my feet. I need answers—answers that won't come to me in the dark, shrouded in the comforts of my cluttered sanctuary. The chill of the apartment wraps around me like a cloak, urging me to seek the warmth of the outside world. I grab my jacket, throw it over my shoulders, and step out into the night.

The air is crisp, biting at my skin but refreshing, invigorating. I wander down the streets of my neighborhood, where the familiar sights feel foreign under the moonlight. Streetlamps cast pools of golden light on the cracked pavement, illuminating the path ahead. I let my feet lead me, driven by an instinct I can't quite name, a magnetic pull toward something greater than myself.

I pass by the coffee shop where Ethan and I spent countless afternoons lost in conversation. The scent of roasting beans and sweet pastries wafts through the air, wrapping around me like a tender embrace. I pause for a moment, memories flooding back—his laughter, the way his eyes sparkled when he shared a joke, the comfort of his presence. But tonight, the shop stands empty, a ghost of the warmth it once held. I turn away, seeking the solace of the lake where I can think without interruption.

The water shimmers under the silvery moon, a tranquil façade hiding the turmoil beneath. I sit on the edge of the dock, my feet dangling over the water's edge. It's eerily quiet, the night wrapped in a heavy stillness that feels almost oppressive. My mind races as I gaze at the reflections on the surface. Each ripple distorts the image, much like my understanding of the reality surrounding me.

Then the phone rings again, shattering the silence like glass breaking. I fumble for it, my heart racing as I recognize the number. It's not Dylan, but I can't bring myself to ignore it. "Hello?" I answer, my voice steadier than I feel.

"Are you alone?" the voice asks, low and steady.

"Who is this?" I demand, irritation bubbling beneath my skin.

"A friend." There's a pause, and I can almost hear the gears turning on the other end. "You're digging too deep, and you might not like what you find."

"Why are you calling me?" My throat feels dry, my pulse quickening with every second that passes.

"Because you need to know the truth, but be careful who you trust," the voice warns before disconnecting, leaving me in a stunned silence. My hand shakes as I lower the phone, the reality of the situation crashing over me like a wave.

What truth? And what does it mean to be careful? I feel like I'm caught in a web, strands of deceit tightening around me with every revelation. I close my eyes, trying to steady my breathing, attempting to pull myself together.

Ethan's words replay in my head, each syllable echoing with a chilling clarity. I need to confront Dylan, to demand answers. But a lingering doubt holds me back. What if I'm not ready to hear what he has to say? What if the truths I uncover shatter the last remnants of my sanity?

My thoughts race as I stand, pacing along the dock's edge, the wooden planks creaking beneath my weight. The moon casts long shadows, flickering against the backdrop of night. I can feel it—a sense of urgency tightening in my chest, propelling me toward a confrontation that feels inevitable.

A sudden rustle in the bushes draws my attention. I freeze, my heart hammering in my chest as I squint into the darkness. My mind flashes back to the cryptic call and the shrouded threats. What if this was more than just a warning? My instincts scream at me to run, but I stand my ground, waiting for whatever comes next.

And then I see him, stepping into the moonlight like a specter. It's Dylan, his expression unreadable, a mask that betrays nothing. "I figured you'd be here," he says, his voice smooth, almost disarmingly calm. "You've always been drawn to the water."

"Why are you here?" I shoot back, the anger bubbling just beneath the surface.

"To talk," he replies, but his tone is laced with a familiarity that sends shivers down my spine. "I think it's time we have a real conversation."

I shake my head, refusing to let him lead me into the depths of his manipulation. "I'm not interested in your lies anymore."

He takes a step closer, the moonlight illuminating his face, casting sharp shadows that dance across his features. "You don't understand. There are things you don't know, and I'm the only one who can help you see them."

The tension between us thickens, a palpable force that draws me in despite my better judgment. I want to hate him, to throw him into the lake and drown him with my anger. But there's a flicker of curiosity—a dangerous spark that ignites the question buried deep within me. What could he possibly reveal that would change everything?

"Look, I'm not interested in whatever game you think this is," I shoot back, trying to maintain my composure even as my insides twist like a tornado. "I'm done playing your little mind tricks."

Dylan tilts his head, that infuriating smirk creeping back onto his face. "And yet, here you are. Out in the middle of the night, waiting for me like a lost puppy. Just admit it, you're curious."

"Curiosity is not the same as trust," I counter, stepping back slightly as if distance might somehow protect me from his influence. "What do you want?"

He sighs dramatically, as if he's about to impart the wisdom of the ages. "You need to understand the game, not just the players. And I'm not the villain you think I am."

I let out a sharp laugh, incredulous. "Oh really? Because last I checked, you're the one who masterminded half the chaos in my life. If that doesn't scream 'villain,' I don't know what does."

"Or maybe I'm just the messenger. The real danger lurks much closer than you realize."

His words hang heavy in the air, and a chill runs down my spine. "What do you mean?"

Dylan takes a step closer, his expression shifting from playful to serious. "There's someone else involved—someone who's been pulling the strings from the shadows. You need to figure out who they are before it's too late."

My heart races as I try to process this revelation. "You expect me to just take your word for it?"

"Trust me or not, but I know what I'm talking about," he says, a hint of desperation breaking through his facade. "You're in over your head, and I can help you navigate it. But you have to be willing to listen."

Against my better judgment, a flicker of interest ignites in me. What could be worse than the betrayal I already know? "Why should I believe you?" I ask, my voice steady even as my pulse quickens.

"Because you've already seen what I'm capable of. And honestly, I'd prefer to help you than watch you flounder."

I snort. "How generous of you."

"Cut the sarcasm. This isn't about you and me. It's bigger than that." He gestures toward the water, as if the lake holds all the answers. "There are pieces you haven't connected yet—truths that will unravel everything you think you know."

"So, enlighten me, oh wise one," I reply, crossing my arms defiantly. "What's your big reveal?"

"I can't tell you everything at once; you wouldn't believe me. But if you come with me, I can show you what I mean."

"Let me guess, you expect me to just hop in your car like a clueless sidekick?"

He shrugs, his expression a mix of frustration and amusement. "Look, it's your choice. But if you want the truth, you might need to take a leap of faith. And I promise I won't bite. Much."

The challenge hangs between us, my instincts screaming at me to run, yet my curiosity ties me in place. There's a glimmer of sincerity in his eyes that I can't quite shake, a vulnerability that feels strangely out of character for the man I thought I knew. "Why now?" I ask, my voice barely above a whisper. "Why are you suddenly so eager to help?"

"I've made mistakes, okay? And maybe I'm tired of watching the people I care about get hurt."

I roll my eyes, skepticism dripping from my tone. "Since when did you start caring?"

"Since I realized how close you were to losing everything," he replies, his voice low, the gravity of his words pulling me closer. "You're smarter than you give yourself credit for. But right now, you're blinded by anger and fear. Trust me; I can help you see the bigger picture."

"By what? Taking me to a secret lair where you and your henchmen plot my downfall?"

His laughter surprises me, bright and unexpected. "I'm not the villain here, and I'd appreciate it if you stopped casting me in that role."

"Fine. Let's say I entertain your little offer. Where exactly are we going?"

"Somewhere we can talk without prying ears. It's not far; I promise."

"What's the catch?"

"Just your company, for now."

I hesitate, torn between the comfort of my familiar life and the uncharted territory ahead. But my desire for clarity pulls me like a siren's call, drawing me toward the unknown. "Fine," I say finally, steeling myself against the rush of uncertainty. "Lead the way."

He grins, and for a moment, the tension dissipates like mist in the morning sun. I follow him down a narrow path leading away from the lake, the trees looming like silent witnesses. The cool breeze whips around us, and I can't shake the feeling that we're venturing into dangerous territory—both literally and figuratively.

As we walk, the silence stretches, filled only with the rustle of leaves and the distant calls of night creatures. I steal glances at Dylan, trying to gauge whether he's genuine or simply weaving another layer of deception. "So, what's your angle?" I ask, breaking the quiet. "What do you get out of this?"

"Redemption, maybe. Or just the chance to fix things before they spiral completely out of control."

I scoff. "That's a noble goal coming from you."

"People can change," he shoots back, his tone sharp. "You should know that better than anyone."

I want to argue, to poke holes in his reasoning, but the truth stabs at me, raw and unyielding. People can change, and sometimes they do it for the better. But that doesn't mean I should trust him—at least, not entirely.

The path opens up into a clearing, illuminated by a cluster of dim lights strung between trees like stars captured in mid-fall. There's an old cabin, the kind that looks like it's been abandoned for years, yet somehow seems alive, beckoning us closer. My heart pounds as we step inside, the scent of aged wood and dust enveloping me like a shroud.

"Welcome to my hideout," Dylan says, a hint of pride in his voice.

"Charming," I mutter, peering into the dim corners as my unease begins to bubble back to the surface.

"Just wait," he urges, leading me to a small table where an array of papers and photographs lay scattered, chaotic yet oddly organized. "This is what I wanted to show you."

As I lean closer, my heart sinks, a heavy weight settling in my stomach. The images are of familiar faces, people I thought I knew, intertwined with strings connecting them like a twisted spider web. A chill runs down my spine as I begin to see the connections, the hidden truths shimmering just beneath the surface.

"Who are these people?" I breathe, the realization dawning on me like a slow, creeping fog.

"Those are the players in the game," Dylan says, his voice low, almost reverent. "And you're right in the center of it all."

Just then, a loud crash echoes from outside, shattering the fragile tension that had settled around us. My heart races as Dylan's eyes widen, and before I can comprehend what's happening, the door bursts open, revealing a figure cloaked in shadows, their intentions obscured by the darkness.

"Dylan!" the figure calls out, voice laced with urgency, sending a wave of dread spiraling through me. "We need to leave—now!"

I glance at Dylan, who looks torn between confusion and fear, and I realize that whatever this is, it's far more dangerous than I ever imagined. The layers of deception I thought I could peel back are only just beginning to unravel, and I'm about to be thrust deeper into the chaos.

Chapter 21: Fractured Reflection

I didn't have to turn around to know it was Ethan. His presence was like a storm cloud, dark and ominous, yet oddly comforting. He had a way of breaking into my solitude without ever really announcing himself, leaving behind an imprint of his urgency. The warmth of the studio had faded with the setting sun, but the air was still thick with the electricity that always buzzed between us, charged with unsaid words and unexamined feelings. I remained rooted in my chair, unwilling to face him just yet, caught in a web of conflicting emotions.

"Still broadcasting the tragedy of your life, I see?" His voice, smooth like aged whiskey, cut through the silence, drawing my attention. I glanced up, finally meeting his gaze. Those deep-set eyes, sharp and searching, held a challenge I was all too familiar with. They had once been a safe harbor; now, they felt like a tempest threatening to drag me under.

"Don't you have better things to do than eavesdrop on my private hell?" I shot back, trying to sound braver than I felt. My bravado felt flimsy, like a spider's web straining against a sudden gust of wind.

"Private hell?" He stepped closer, his silhouette outlined by the faint glow of the control panel. "You make it sound so poetic. But really, it's just a tragicomic mess, isn't it?"

I scoffed, rolling my eyes, but inside, I felt the familiar pang of discomfort that his words stirred. He had a knack for stripping away my defenses, leaving me raw and exposed. "You think you're clever, don't you?"

"I think you're too good at hiding," he replied, his tone suddenly serious. "You act like you have it all figured out, but the cracks are showing, and I'm not the only one who's noticed."

I leaned back in my chair, crossing my arms defensively. "You don't know anything about me."

"Is that what you tell yourself?" he countered, taking another step forward, the space between us shrinking. "You're a master of disguise, but I see the way your hands tremble when the calls come in. You're terrified."

"Maybe I am." I swallowed hard, the admission tasting bitter on my tongue. "Maybe I'm terrified of you."

"Of me?" A wry smile crept across his lips, a mixture of amusement and something softer that flickered in his eyes. "That's flattering. But really, you should be terrified of the choices you're making. Trusting the wrong people, believing in their twisted narratives."

"What do you want from me, Ethan?" I burst out, the frustration boiling over. "I'm not some pawn in your game. I'm not a project to be fixed."

"I never said you were," he said gently, his voice dropping to a conspiratorial whisper. "But you keep playing the role of the victim, and it's exhausting to watch. You don't have to be strong all the time, you know."

I stared at him, incredulous. "And what makes you the expert on strength? You're the one who walked away when things got complicated."

His expression hardened for a moment, the truth of my words hitting home. But just as quickly, the warmth returned, and he leaned against the doorframe, an image of casual defiance. "I was trying to protect you from the fallout of my mistakes. But now, it feels like I should have stayed. Maybe then you wouldn't be so lost."

"Lost? I'm not lost; I'm just..." I trailed off, frustration morphing into vulnerability. "I'm just trying to find a way to be me again. Without the noise, without the expectations."

Ethan stepped forward, bridging the gap between us, and for a heartbeat, I could feel the weight of his presence pulling me toward him, urging me to let go of the fear that had built its fortress inside me. "Then stop performing. Just be."

"Just be?" I laughed bitterly, the sound echoing in the empty studio. "That's rich coming from you. How many times have you told me to keep it together? To keep the show running?"

"Because you were drowning," he said softly. "You think I didn't notice how the spotlight dimmed your shine? How you faded behind that microphone? You're meant to be more than this." He gestured around the room, at the soundboard, at the walls that had witnessed my laughter and my tears, my dreams and my nightmares.

"More than this?" I echoed, the words heavy with the weight of their implications. "What does that even mean? More than a voice on the radio? More than the woman who's made a career out of her brokenness?"

Ethan's gaze locked onto mine, fierce and unyielding. "It means being the woman I know you are. The one who isn't afraid to confront her demons, to fight for what she wants. You're more than a victim of circumstance; you're a survivor. And you need to remember that."

"I don't know how," I admitted, my voice trembling. "I don't know how to stop being what everyone expects me to be."

"Then let me help you," he offered, his sincerity cutting through the tension like a knife through the thick fog of doubt that surrounded me. "Stop pretending you're fine. Let me in, and maybe we can figure this out together."

I hesitated, the gravity of his words weighing heavily on me. The idea of vulnerability was terrifying, yet enticing—a whisper of hope in a world filled with shadows. "Together?" I questioned, the word tasting strange on my tongue.

"Yes, together." He stepped even closer, the warmth of his body radiating toward me, drawing me in like gravity. "You're not alone in this. You never were."

"What's the matter, you look like you just survived a natural disaster," Ethan remarked, tilting his head slightly as he surveyed the chaos that had become my sanctuary. The teasing lilt in his voice held a thread of concern that tugged at something deep within me.

"I might as well have," I retorted, rolling my eyes. "And here you are, a harbinger of further calamity. Thanks for that."

His chuckle was soft, rich with a warmth that seemed to counter the chill in the room. "You're the one who looks like she could use a lifeline. Maybe even a rescue mission."

"Is that your plan? To swoop in and save me?" I countered, a mix of sarcasm and genuine curiosity weaving through my tone. "I thought that sort of thing went out of style with chivalry."

"Hey, I might not be a knight in shining armor," he said, crossing his arms, a flicker of mischief in his eyes, "but I've got a decent set of tools in my metaphorical utility belt. We could put them to good use."

A reluctant smile tugged at my lips. "What are you suggesting? A DIY project to fix my shattered psyche?"

"Absolutely," he replied, stepping closer, his expression serious yet playful. "First, we start by stripping away the layers of paint and despair, and then we'll see what we're working with. I'm betting there's something beautiful beneath all that mess."

I let out a laugh, the tension in my shoulders easing slightly. "You think I'm hiding beauty? Please, I'm pretty sure I'm more of a fixer-upper than a hidden gem."

Ethan's gaze turned intense, and the air between us thickened. "You're more than you give yourself credit for. You just need to believe it."

As much as I wanted to dismiss his earnestness, something about his conviction reached me. I looked down at my hands, still trembling slightly, a constant reminder of the emotional storm raging inside me. "It's hard to see beauty when you feel so broken," I murmured, the words spilling out before I could stop them.

"Then let me help you piece it back together," he urged, his voice low and steady. "One shard at a time. You don't have to do this alone."

The vulnerability in his offer hung in the air, a fragile thread binding us. I could feel my heart racing, caught between the desire to let him in and the instinct to shut him out. "You're going to regret this," I warned, half-joking, half-serious. "I'm not exactly a walk in the park."

"Trust me, I've navigated worse terrain." His grin was infectious, and for a moment, I felt lighter, as if the weight of my fears had lifted just a fraction.

"I could use a little more trust and a little less disaster in my life," I admitted, meeting his gaze again. "But what if I'm not salvageable? What if this is as good as it gets?"

Ethan stepped forward, closing the distance, his presence enveloping me in a sense of safety I hadn't realized I craved. "Then we'll redefine what 'good' looks like. Besides, there's a certain charm in being a little broken, don't you think? It makes for great stories."

"Great stories," I echoed, a hint of irony creeping into my voice. "You mean like the one where I become the poster child for emotional instability?"

"More like the one where you overcome it. Think of the plot twist!" he exclaimed, his enthusiasm bubbling over. "The heroine doesn't just accept her flaws; she embraces them, uses them to fuel her fire. It's all about how you choose to narrate your life."

"Is that how you see me? As some kind of heroine?" I asked, surprised by the way the word ignited a spark of hope within me.

"Absolutely," he said without hesitation. "You just need to find your voice again. The one that doesn't rely on others' expectations."

The sincerity in his eyes ignited a flicker of something in me, a warmth I hadn't felt in what seemed like ages. "Okay," I said, allowing myself to breathe. "But where do I start?"

"Start by acknowledging what you want. Not what everyone else wants. What do you really want?" He leaned in closer, the warmth of his presence wrapping around me like a comfort blanket.

"I want..." My voice faltered as I wrestled with the truth that had been buried beneath layers of fear and doubt. "I want to feel whole again. To not wake up every morning wondering who I am. To stop pretending that everything's fine when it's not."

Ethan's expression softened, and for a brief moment, I caught a glimpse of the man behind the bravado—the one who understood that even the strongest among us sometimes crumbled under the weight of our burdens. "Then let's chase that together. One step at a time."

Just as I felt the flicker of hope catch fire, the ringing of my phone shattered the moment. The shrill sound pierced through the air, reverberating in the silence of the studio. I hesitated, my heart pounding, unsure whether to answer or let it go to voicemail.

Ethan glanced at the screen, then back at me, his brow furrowing slightly. "You going to get that?"

I shook my head, the anxiety creeping back in. "It's probably just Dylan, or someone else trying to pull me into their chaos."

"Then let them wait. You're here right now. Focus on what's in front of you." His gaze held mine, steady and unwavering, but the phone continued to ring, each tone echoing in my mind like a siren song I couldn't ignore.

Finally, I relented, reaching for the phone, the dread coiling tighter in my stomach. "What if it's important?" I muttered, even as I knew it wasn't. It was just another tether pulling me back into the turmoil I was trying to escape.

"Then you'll handle it. You're stronger than you think," Ethan encouraged, but his voice held a hint of apprehension as I swiped to answer.

"Hello?" I said, my voice barely a whisper, uncertainty creeping into my tone.

"Is this Amelia?" The voice on the other end was unfamiliar, smooth but laced with an undercurrent of urgency. "We need to talk. It's about Dylan."

The blood drained from my face as the implications of the statement washed over me. My heart raced, and the room seemed to close in around me. "What about him?" I asked, my voice steadier than I felt.

"It's urgent. We need to meet."

As the words sank in, the shadows of the past loomed larger than ever, threatening to swallow me whole. "No, I can't—"

Ethan's hand on my arm stopped me, his touch grounding me in the chaos. "Amelia, you don't have to do this alone," he urged, his voice fierce yet gentle.

The line went dead, the echo of the voice still reverberating in my ears. I looked at Ethan, panic flickering in my chest. "What do I do?"

The fear in my voice made him step closer, but as he opened his mouth to speak, my phone buzzed violently again, a familiar number lighting up the screen. Dylan.

And with that, the world felt like it was unraveling once more, my grip on reality slipping through my fingers like sand.

Chapter 22: Face to Face

Dylan stands in the doorway, the dim light from the hallway casting long shadows across his face. My heart lurches, a sickening combination of fear and anger rising in my chest. He looks calm, too calm, as if he's been waiting for this moment for years. And maybe he has.

For a moment, neither of us speaks. The weight of everything unsaid hangs heavy between us. I want to scream at him, demand answers, but the words catch in my throat. It's Dylan who breaks the silence first, his voice soft, almost apologetic. "I didn't want it to come to this," he says, stepping closer, his presence suffocating.

I don't let him get any closer. I stand, fists clenched at my sides, every muscle in my body tense. "You've been playing me for years," I spit, my voice shaking with rage. "Why?"

Dylan's expression shifts, a flicker of something dark passing over his features. "Because I had to," he says, his voice barely above a whisper. "You don't understand what's at stake."

"What's at stake?" I bark, my laughter tinged with disbelief. "The truth, Dylan. That's what's at stake. You've been lying to me, manipulating everything like it's some twisted game. I refuse to play anymore."

He takes a step back, surprise flaring in his eyes as if I've slapped him. "It was never a game, Alice," he says, trying to sound earnest, but it falls flat against the backdrop of my fury. "I was trying to protect you."

"Protect me? Or protect yourself?" I challenge, voice rising with every word. My heart thunders like a war drum, echoing the battle raging in my mind. Each memory of stolen glances, whispered secrets, and shared laughter now feels like a betrayal, a facade crafted from smoke and mirrors.

Dylan runs a hand through his hair, frustration etching deeper lines into his forehead. "You think I wanted any of this? You think I wanted to hurt you?" His voice cracks, revealing the slightest hint of vulnerability, but it does little to soften my resolve.

"No, you wanted to control me. You wanted me to dance to your tune while you pulled the strings." I advance, refusing to cower beneath the weight of his gaze. "I trusted you, Dylan. I believed you when you told me everything would be okay. But all I see now is your shadow lurking behind every promise."

His eyes flash with something—regret, anger, or perhaps a mixture of both—but he remains silent, caught in the crossfire of my accusations. The air between us thickens, charged with unspoken words and unresolved emotions. It's almost palpable, a current of energy that pulls and pushes like the tide, leaving us stranded in the wreckage of what could have been.

"Is this how you planned it?" I demand, my voice dropping to a whisper as the enormity of the situation washes over me. "To let me fall, to make me think we were real when you were just waiting for the right moment to pull the rug out from under me?"

He clenches his jaw, muscles tensing as if he's bracing for impact. "No. I never wanted to hurt you. I thought if I could just keep you safe long enough, maybe it would all work out."

"Safe?" I echo incredulously. "You thought lying would keep me safe? Keeping secrets is what put me in danger, Dylan! You've put me in danger!" My hands tremble at my sides, and I fight the urge to reach out and shake him until the truth falls from his lips like marbles rolling across the floor.

The silence stretches between us, and I can almost hear the clock ticking, each second marking the distance between who we were and who we are now. Finally, he speaks, the words heavy with a weight I can't comprehend. "There are things you don't know, Alice. Things that could change everything."

"Then tell me!" I shout, my voice cracking under the pressure of my desperation. "Tell me everything, or I swear I'll walk away, and I won't look back."

For a brief moment, his resolve falters. I can see the internal battle raging behind his eyes, the turmoil of a man torn between loyalty and truth. He takes a deep breath, a long sigh that seems to deflate the tension in the room just enough to create a crack in the wall he's built around himself.

"I can't," he admits, voice low and strained. "Not like this. You don't understand the consequences."

"Consequences? For whom? Because it sure as hell feels like I'm the one bearing the weight of your choices."

"Everything I've done has been for you." He steps forward, and I'm almost surprised by the intensity of his gaze. "The decisions I made, the paths I chose—none of it was easy. But I thought, if I could just keep you in the dark a little longer, I could protect you from the fallout."

"From what? From the truth?" I shake my head, feeling a whirlwind of emotions threatening to overwhelm me. "You think you're protecting me by keeping me in the dark? All you're doing is making me feel like a fool."

Dylan's face twists, his frustration boiling to the surface. "You think this is easy for me? You think I wanted to lie to you? I wanted to tell you everything, but it's complicated. There are people who could get hurt. Real people."

"People? Or just your precious secrets?"

He falters, and for a brief moment, I think he might finally break. But instead, he retreats behind his walls, the familiar mask slipping back into place. "You wouldn't understand, Alice. You're not ready to hear it."

The challenge in his eyes only fuels my anger. "Try me. I'm done being in the dark. It's your move, Dylan. Either you trust me enough to share what you're hiding or you let me walk away from this once and for all."

As the silence stretches painfully between us again, I can feel the world outside our little bubble—cars rushing by, laughter echoing from the streets, the distant sound of music playing somewhere nearby. It's a vivid reminder that life continues on, even as we remain suspended in this moment of confrontation. I refuse to back down.

I take a step back, the air between us thickening, charged with the weight of his admission. "What's at stake? Your precious reputation?" I bite back, unable to mask the venom in my tone. "Or is it just the secret you've been nursing like a prized possession?"

Dylan's brow furrows, a mixture of frustration and something deeper swirling in his gaze. "You don't get it. This isn't just about us. It never was." His voice grows stronger, tinged with an urgency that grabs my attention. "There are forces at play that you can't begin to comprehend, and I didn't want you dragged into this."

"Oh, I'm already dragged in, Dylan," I retort, gesturing wildly around the room. "I'm neck-deep in your mess whether I want to be or not. So enlighten me. What dark secret has you so terrified?"

He hesitates, chewing on his lower lip as if weighing the consequences of his words. It's maddening, watching him wrestle with his own truth, while I stand here, desperate for clarity. "There are people who want to control you," he finally admits, each word deliberate, as if he's testing their strength. "People who don't care about your life. They care about what you can do for them."

"Control me? What are you talking about?" My heart races, the beat echoing in my ears like a warning bell. "Who are these people?"

A shadow flickers across his face, and I catch a glimpse of the boy I fell for—a boy who, at one point, had a sense of humor that could lighten the heaviest of moments. The change in his demeanor feels like a jolt, a reminder that beneath this façade of calm lies a tempest of turmoil. "They're not just people, Alice. They're part of something bigger. A web of deceit that runs deeper than you know."

"Now you're talking in riddles. Is this a spy movie I've accidentally stumbled into?" I scoff, trying to diffuse the tension with humor, but it lands flat in the heavy air. "Why not just lay it all out? Is it a contract with a demon? Or maybe an alien conspiracy? Come on, spill it."

His eyes darken, and I realize I've crossed a line. "You think this is a joke?" he snaps, the fire igniting in his tone, forcing me to take a step back. "This is serious, Alice. They're watching you, and if you don't take this seriously, you'll be caught in the crossfire."

"Watching me? Who?" I demand, feeling the ground shift beneath my feet. The playful banter I'm used to suddenly feels inappropriate, like a clown at a funeral.

His silence is answer enough. I can feel the pit of dread grow heavier in my stomach as pieces of a puzzle I didn't even know existed start to drift into place. "Dylan, tell me you're joking," I plead, but the look on his face is anything but playful.

"Do you think I'd joke about something like this?" he replies, his voice steady but laced with an edge that sends chills up my spine. "You need to trust me. I'm trying to protect you from a world you're not ready for."

"Protect me? By lying? By keeping me in the dark? Do you think that's going to help?" The anger resurges, roaring to life like a flame caught in a gust of wind. "I can't believe you. I want to trust you, but you make it impossible!"

"You're right," he concedes, rubbing the back of his neck in a gesture that betrays his anxiety. "I made mistakes. But you need to understand, I was trying to keep you safe from the truth, from this mess. And now it's too late. They know about you."

"Who knows about me?" Panic seeps into my voice. "You have to give me something to work with here."

He takes a step closer, and I can see the conflict etched into his features. "I should have told you sooner," he murmurs, the gravity of his confession hanging between us like a thick fog. "There are people who would do anything to get what they want. You're not just some girl to them; you're a key to a door they want to unlock."

"A key?" My mind races, trying to make sense of the chaos swirling around us. "What kind of door?"

"The kind that leads to power. Information. Control over everything. They want you because of what you know, what you've been exposed to." He pauses, eyes locking onto mine with a fierce intensity. "You have to leave. Now."

"Leave? Just like that?" I laugh, a sharp, bitter sound that echoes off the walls. "And go where? Away from you? Away from everything I've built? You can't be serious."

"I'm dead serious." His eyes blaze, a mixture of desperation and urgency radiating from him. "You need to understand the stakes here. They'll use you, and once they're done, they won't think twice about tossing you aside. You're too valuable to them."

"I'm not some pawn in your game, Dylan!" I shout, the tears I've been holding back spilling over. "I refuse to run away because you think I'm in danger! I want to stand my ground and face whatever's coming, even if it means taking risks."

"But it's not just your life at stake anymore," he replies, his voice a low growl, a desperate plea for reason. "They'll come for you. They'll come for anyone connected to you. I can't let that happen."

"What if I want to be connected to you?" The words slip out before I can stop them, raw and unfiltered. "You're telling me to run, but I don't want to run away from you. I want to fight with you."

He steps back, the distance between us growing as he struggles with his own feelings. "You don't know what you're saying, Alice. You don't realize how deep this runs."

"Then show me. Show me the truth, and maybe I can understand," I insist, voice trembling with conviction. "You owe me that much."

The moment stretches, suspended in time, as the weight of our choices settles over us like a thick blanket. Dylan's gaze flickers, uncertainty clouding his eyes. "If I tell you, you might not be able to come back from it," he warns, the tension building in the air.

"Then let me decide," I reply, my heart pounding like a war drum. "I deserve to know the risks."

The look he gives me is heavy, filled with a mixture of dread and longing. It feels like we're standing on the edge of a precipice, teetering on the brink of the unknown. "You're sure about this?" he asks, the gravity of the moment weighing heavily on both of us.

"I am," I say, firm in my resolve. "I want the truth, Dylan. Give it to me."

He swallows hard, his throat working as if the words are stuck there, fighting to escape. Just as he opens his mouth to speak, the sudden sound of a door slamming echoes from the hallway, jolting us both. A flash of movement darts past the crack beneath the door, and I feel the room grow colder, the air thickening with an unspoken dread.

Dylan's expression shifts, panic rising in his eyes. "We're not alone," he breathes, and my heart sinks as I realize the truth.

The moment before the world tilts, the tension snaps, and I know we've crossed a line we can't uncross. Just as the door bursts open, and a figure looms in the entrance, everything I thought I knew begins to unravel, leaving me staring into the abyss of a dark, uncertain future.

Chapter 23: Lines in the Sand

Dylan leans against the doorframe, arms crossed as if he's guarding some invisible treasure. His posture is relaxed, but the tension rippling just beneath the surface tells me he's anything but at ease. I can feel my heart thumping wildly in my chest, each pulse screaming for clarity, for some semblance of control in a situation that has spiraled into chaos.

"Important?" I echo, letting the word hang in the air like a thick fog. It feels like a trap, a word carefully chosen to provoke curiosity rather than offer any real insight. "What do you mean by that? What could I possibly have that anyone would want?"

His gaze narrows, and for a fleeting moment, I see something flicker behind his cool facade—a hint of regret, maybe? But it vanishes before I can grasp it, replaced by the calculating look that has come to define him in my mind.

"You're too smart for your own good, you know that?" he says, a smirk creeping onto his lips, and for a heartbeat, I'm reminded of the man I thought I knew—the charming guy with the easy laugh, who could make the sun feel like it was shining just a little brighter. "You have a gift, a talent for understanding things most people can't even begin to grasp. That's why they're watching you. They need you."

A bitter laugh escapes my lips, sharp enough to cut through the tension. "Need me for what? A puppet show?" I shake my head, dismissing the notion as if it's a foul odor lingering in the air. "I'm not a pawn in your little game, Dylan. I'm not interested in being used or manipulated."

"Not a pawn, no. A queen, perhaps," he counters smoothly, his tone laced with a mix of flattery and something darker. "You're not just an afterthought. They see potential in you, potential that could change everything."

"Everything?" I scoff, unable to contain my disbelief. "This isn't some grand narrative, Dylan. This is my life, and it's falling apart. If

I'm the queen, I must have missed the memo about the kingdom being under siege."

His smirk falters, and for the first time, I see genuine frustration flicker across his features. "You're playing a dangerous game, you know. Ignoring the reality of the situation only makes it worse."

With a quick intake of breath, I force myself to stand tall, even as uncertainty churns within me. "And what reality is that? The one where I'm supposed to trust you? The one where my life is up for grabs because some faceless people have decided I'm 'important'?"

"Faceless?" he repeats, his eyes glinting like a predator's. "That's the problem, isn't it? You're too close to the truth to see how deep the rabbit hole goes. It's not just about you anymore. It's about power, influence, and how much you're willing to risk to find out what that really means."

Power. The word rolls off his tongue like honey, sweet but sticky, dangerous. "So, what do you want from me, Dylan? Am I supposed to play your little game? Put on a crown and play the queen? Or am I just a means to an end?"

His silence stretches, thickening the air between us until it crackles with tension. "I want you to understand the stakes," he finally says, his voice low and steady. "This isn't about me or you; it's bigger than both of us. You have a role to play, whether you like it or not."

I lean back against the desk, arms crossed defensively. The surface is cool against my skin, a stark contrast to the heat rising in my chest. "And if I refuse?"

Dylan pushes off the wall, his gaze piercing as he steps closer, invading my space with a confidence that feels suffocating. "Then you risk losing everything—your life, your freedom. They won't just walk away. You're a target now."

"Great," I reply, my voice dripping with sarcasm, trying to mask the rising tide of fear that threatens to swallow me whole. "Just what I always wanted. To be a target."

"Look, I know it sounds insane," he concedes, running a hand through his hair in frustration, a gesture that feels oddly vulnerable in this charged moment. "But trust me, I'm not the enemy here. I'm trying to protect you. This is bigger than you think."

I shake my head, disbelief coiling tight in my chest. "Protect me? By dragging me into your chaos? I'd rather take my chances alone."

"Alone?" he laughs bitterly, the sound reverberating in the cramped room like a ghost haunting my resolve. "You think you can walk away from this? You think they'll let you?"

His words hang in the air, weighty and menacing. Suddenly, the reality of my situation sinks in deeper, each realization more chilling than the last. I'm not just caught in a web of deceit; I'm at the center of something much darker, and the strands are tightening around me.

"I'm done playing your games, Dylan," I say, my voice firmer than I feel. "I want out."

He steps back, a flicker of surprise crossing his features before it hardens into something unreadable. "You don't get to choose that. It's not just about you anymore."

The walls feel like they're closing in, the weight of his words pressing down on me like a suffocating blanket. There's a storm brewing in my chest, a tempest of anger and fear colliding with the lingering remnants of a trust that's been shredded to pieces.

"Tell me what I need to do," I demand, the defiance spilling out of me like a wave crashing against the shore. "If I'm as important as you say, then I need to know what I'm up against. You owe me that."

Dylan regards me with a mixture of admiration and caution, the silence stretching between us like a taut wire, ready to snap. "Fine," he replies at last, his voice dropping to a conspiratorial whisper. "But know this: once you step into the light, there's no turning back."

With those words, the ground shifts beneath my feet, and I'm left standing on the precipice of something terrifying and exhilarating, a tangled web of fate that I can't begin to comprehend.

My breath catches as the implications of his words settle like a heavy fog, blurring the boundaries of reality. The very thought of being important—of having anyone watch me with intent—is absurd. A shiver races down my spine, igniting a blend of dread and curiosity that wraps around my thoughts like a vice.

"Important?" I repeat, struggling to keep my voice steady. "To who? And why? I'm just... me." The weight of my insignificance feels palpable, yet Dylan stands there, leaning into the shadows like a bad actor in a play too far removed from its script.

He steps closer, the distance between us shrinking, creating a tension that sizzles in the air. "You're not just 'you' anymore," he states, his tone dropping, almost conspiratorial. "You're part of something much larger. And I'm here to help you navigate it."

"Help?" I scoff, disbelief turning my words sharp. "Is that what we're calling this? Because it feels more like a trap."

A smirk plays on his lips, and I can't help but notice how his dark charm is as disarming as it is infuriating. "You know me better than that. I wouldn't put you in danger without a solid reason."

"Solid reason?" I shake my head, a bitter laugh escaping my lips. "Dylan, the last time I checked, I was running for my life, not collecting tokens for a scavenger hunt."

"Exactly," he replies, his intensity sharpening. "And that's why you need to understand who you're dealing with. There are forces at play that are willing to go to extremes to get what they want. They won't hesitate to use you as leverage."

"Leverage," I echo, the word tasting sour. "So you admit it. I'm just a pawn to you and your mysterious 'they.'"

"Not just a pawn—a key," he corrects, his expression suddenly earnest. "You hold answers they're desperate for, and they'll do anything to get to you."

My pulse quickens, panic creeping in with icy fingers. "What answers? I don't have anything of value. I'm just trying to make sense of this mess."

He leans in, lowering his voice like we're sharing a dark secret, and the intimacy of the moment sends a jolt through me. "You don't even know what you know," he whispers, his gaze locking onto mine with an intensity that makes my skin prickle. "It's buried beneath layers of confusion and fear, but it's there. I can help you uncover it."

"Why would you want to help me?" I ask, a hint of vulnerability breaking through my defiance. "After everything?"

"Because I'm not the enemy," he insists, a flash of frustration in his eyes. "I was wrong, yes, but I want to set things right. This is about survival, yours and mine."

"Right," I scoff, folding my arms tightly across my chest, trying to shield myself from the reality closing in. "And I suppose you'll do that by dragging me deeper into whatever rabbit hole you've fallen into?"

He shrugs, a glimmer of a smile returning to his lips, though it feels more like a mask than anything genuine. "Not dragging. Guiding. Trust me, I know this world. I've made mistakes, but I can help you avoid the same traps."

"Why should I trust you?"

"Because," he replies, the laughter gone from his voice, replaced by something more serious. "What choice do you have? You can fight me, or you can fight with me. Either way, we need to figure out who's pulling the strings before they find you first."

The room grows silent, and in that silence, I feel the weight of my uncertainty settle heavily on my shoulders. What did I really know about Dylan, anyway? The man standing before me was an enigma wrapped in contradictions, a puppet master who claimed to want to help but was as much a part of the problem as the forces he spoke of.

I turn my back to him, staring out the window at the rain-drenched street below. Each droplet feels like a tear shed for the life I used to know—a life filled with simple worries and mundane routines. Now, it's as if I've stepped onto a precarious tightrope, the ground below a swirling abyss of unknown dangers.

"I don't want to be part of your game," I say quietly, but the resolve in my voice falters.

"It's not a game, and you're already part of it," he replies, and when I turn back to face him, I see that flicker of determination in his eyes that makes my heart race with something between fear and intrigue. "You need to accept that. The only way out is through."

"Fine," I concede, crossing my arms tighter as if that might shield me from the reality swirling around us. "What's the plan?"

He steps forward, a spark of something—hope? Desperation?—lighting his features. "We start by finding out exactly what they know. We'll dig deep, and we'll do it together. No more secrets."

"Together," I echo, the weight of the word hanging between us, ripe with possibilities and dangers. "And if I decide to bail?"

"Then you'll be walking into the jaws of something far worse than you can imagine." His voice drops to a whisper, almost intimate. "You're already in too deep. You can't run now."

"Charming," I murmur, rolling my eyes but feeling the spark of adrenaline beneath my skin. "So, what's next? A late-night rendezvous with a shadowy figure?"

"Actually, yes," he replies, a glimmer of mischief returning to his gaze. "But first, we need to get you out of here."

Before I can question what he means, he reaches for my wrist, pulling me gently but firmly towards the door. "Trust me. We need to move quickly."

As we step into the dimly lit hallway, my heart races—not just from fear, but from the thrill of uncertainty, of diving headfirst into a mystery that could consume me whole. The shadows loom larger as we navigate the tight corridors, each step taking me further from safety and deeper into a world I barely comprehend.

Just as we reach the exit, a loud crash echoes from the floor above us, reverberating through the building like an alarm bell. My heart drops, and I freeze, dread pooling in my stomach.

"What was that?" I whisper, my voice trembling with the realization that we may not be alone.

Dylan's expression shifts, a dark determination flaring in his eyes. "We need to go. Now."

As we sprint towards the exit, the sound of footsteps echoes behind us, heavy and relentless. The thrill of the chase ignites a fire within me, and for the first time, I can't help but feel a surge of adrenaline pushing me forward.

But the thrill is short-lived as I glance back, and there, emerging from the shadows, is a figure I never expected to see—a face I thought I had left behind. A smirk plays on their lips, as if they've been waiting for this moment all along.

"Did you really think you could escape?" they taunt, their voice dripping with malice, sending a chill down my spine.

And just like that, I realize this was only the beginning of a far more dangerous game, one that has only just begun to unfold.

Chapter 24: The Ties That Bind

The sunlight filters through the half-drawn curtains, casting a delicate lacework of shadows across the walls, but I barely notice. My mind is tangled in the chaos Dylan left behind. It's like a storm has rolled through my life, uprooting everything familiar and leaving a wake of uncertainty. I can feel Ethan's gaze lingering on me, his expression a mixture of worry and something deeper—something I'm still too muddled to decipher.

"I've spent years trying to figure things out," I admit, the words slipping out before I can catch them. "Every day felt like a puzzle I was meant to solve. And now, it feels like the pieces were never even mine to begin with."

Ethan shifts in his seat, the old leather couch creaking under the weight of unspoken thoughts. He runs a hand through his messy hair, a habit I've always found charming. "You don't have to go through this alone," he says softly. "Whatever Dylan is mixed up in, you've got people who care about you. We'll figure it out together."

The warmth in his voice wraps around me like a well-worn blanket, comforting yet heavy with expectation. I want to believe him, to let go of the weight pressing down on my chest, but the shadows of Dylan's words cling stubbornly. "But what if this is bigger than us? What if I'm in over my head?" I counter, biting my lip.

He leans forward, his eyes narrowing as he considers my fear. "Sometimes, the only way to break free from someone else's script is to write your own ending." The conviction in his voice makes my heart race, and I feel a flicker of hope beneath the layers of doubt.

A sharp knock at the door interrupts our moment. Ethan's brows knit together, and he stands, glancing at me. "Stay here," he instructs, his voice firm. I nod, the pit in my stomach tightening as I watch him approach the door. The abruptness of it all sends adrenaline coursing through my veins.

He peeks through the peephole and frowns, opening the door just a crack. "What do you want?" he asks, his tone shifting from confusion to guardedness. I can't hear the voice on the other side, but I can see the shadow—tall and familiar.

"Ethan," the voice calls, smooth yet laced with urgency. "I need to talk to you. It's about her."

Panic tightens my chest as I strain to listen, curiosity pulling me closer to the door. The mention of me sets off alarms in my head. "Who is it?" I whisper, but Ethan motions for silence, his expression shifting from concern to something that feels dangerously close to dread.

He opens the door wider, and in steps a figure who sends a jolt of recognition through me. It's Noah, a friend from college with a smile that once could light up a room, now twisted by the weight of something he's carrying. "We need to get you out of here," he says, his voice low but urgent. "There's been a development, and it's not good."

"Development?" I echo, my heart pounding in my ears.

"Can we talk privately?" Noah glances back at me, then at Ethan. The tension is palpable, and I can sense the change in the air, like an approaching storm.

Ethan crosses his arms, narrowing his eyes. "I don't think you understand the situation," he replies, his tone protective. "She just found out some serious stuff. If you're here to drop more bombshells—"

"No, listen!" Noah interrupts, raising his hands in a placating gesture. "I'm not here to add to her stress. I'm here to keep her safe. We're not just talking about Dylan anymore."

The weight of his words settles heavily between us, and I find my voice, laced with defiance. "What do you mean, 'not just Dylan'? Who else is involved?"

Noah glances at Ethan, then back at me, the vulnerability in his gaze stark against his usual bravado. "It's complicated. There's a group—people who've been watching you. They're not just observers;

they're planning something. I thought you should know before it's too late."

"Planning what?" I ask, my stomach dropping.

"It's hard to explain," Noah says, shifting on his feet as if the weight of my gaze is too much. "They're interested in your... potential. There's something about you that they think can be used."

"Used?" The word feels heavy, a stone lodged in my throat. "What does that even mean?"

"Listen, I didn't come here to scare you," Noah insists, his voice steadying. "But if Dylan is involved, that's a bad sign. He's always been a wildcard. If he's leading you into something, you need to be prepared."

Ethan takes a step closer to me, his protective instinct flaring. "We can handle this together," he says, shooting Noah a hard look. "But I need you to explain everything, and fast."

"Noah," I add, my voice steadier than I feel. "You've got to tell me the truth. If there's a group out there watching me, I can't ignore it."

"Fine," Noah concedes, the weight of the world pressing down on his shoulders. "But you need to trust me. I'll tell you everything, but we have to move. There are eyes everywhere."

In that moment, my heart thrums with a mix of fear and anticipation. I've always prided myself on being in control, but here I am, in a whirlwind of uncertainty, my world spinning faster than I can grasp. As Noah shares fragments of a story I can hardly comprehend, I can't shake the feeling that this is just the beginning.

As Noah continues to spill secrets in rapid-fire bursts, I feel the walls of Ethan's apartment closing in, the air thickening with the weight of revelations. "You don't understand," Noah insists, running a hand through his hair in frustration. "This isn't just some petty jealousy from Dylan. This is serious. There are people who believe you hold some key to whatever their agenda is."

"Agenda?" I repeat, struggling to wrap my head around the concept. "What agenda? I'm just... me."

Ethan interjects, his voice steady but edged with concern. "Noah, we need specifics. What exactly are they planning? Are they a threat?"

Noah glances around the cramped space, as if the very walls might have ears. "They're a shadowy organization. I don't know who's leading it, but they've been involved in some questionable activities. I just found out they've been tracking you for months. I thought you were safe—until I realized how much they know."

The chill of his words seeps into my bones. "Safe?" I scoff, the irony cutting sharp. "I haven't felt safe in weeks. What do they want from me? Is this some sort of game?"

"It's not a game," Noah insists, urgency crackling in his voice. "It's bigger than that. They're not just after you—they're after something you might not even know you have."

A silence falls, thick as fog, punctuated only by the ticking of the clock on the wall. I can almost hear the gears turning in my head, each tick a reminder of time slipping away. "What if this is about Dylan?" I ask, hesitantly. "What if he's leading them to me? What if he's already pulled me into whatever this is?"

Noah shakes his head. "Dylan is a piece of the puzzle, not the whole picture. He's impulsive, dangerous even, but he's also a pawn. You've got to realize, the stakes are much higher."

My heart races. "What does that even mean? How do I fit into their plans? I'm just a barista with a penchant for bad choices and a questionable taste in men."

"Believe it or not," Ethan chimes in, his tone almost teasing, "that might be exactly what makes you so interesting to them. You're underestimating yourself."

"Gee, thanks," I shoot back, crossing my arms defensively. "What I really need is a fan club right now."

Noah gives a half-smile, but it quickly fades. "Look, we need to act fast. They could make a move at any moment. You should come with me, lay low for a while."

"Lay low?" I repeat incredulously. "Do I look like I'm capable of stealth? I can't even manage to hide my emotions from a coffee cup!"

"You might have to learn," Noah replies, his tone suddenly serious. "They know your patterns, your routines. If we can disrupt that, it might buy us some time. You can't stay here; it's too risky."

Ethan's eyes dart between us, concern etching deeper lines on his forehead. "Noah, this is insane. We can't just uproot her life without a plan. What if they come after her anyway? What if they know she's with you?"

"They might," Noah concedes, a frown tugging at his lips. "But it's a risk we have to take. We need to keep you one step ahead."

I feel the walls closing in again, the enormity of it all pressing down. "You're talking about running. Like, really running?"

Noah nods, his gaze unwavering. "It's not about fear; it's about survival. We can't let them control your narrative any longer."

"I didn't even want a narrative!" I exclaim, feeling frustration bubble up inside me. "I just wanted a quiet life with my lattes and the occasional awkward date. Now I'm wrapped up in whatever this is?"

"Welcome to the club," Ethan murmurs, trying to lighten the mood, but his eyes betray the seriousness of our situation. "I never signed up for this either."

"Right? It's a terrible membership deal," I quip, trying to shake the rising tide of anxiety. "But really, what am I supposed to do? I'm not cut out for spy games or whatever this is."

"Just follow our lead," Noah replies, his tone coaxing. "We'll figure it out as we go. You have a strength you might not even realize. Trust me."

I stare at him, trying to read the sincerity in his eyes. I want to trust him, to believe that he knows what he's doing. But the truth hangs heavy in the air like a storm cloud, and my gut twists with unease. "And if I say no?"

"Then we risk letting them find you before we can protect you," Noah says, the gravity of his words landing like a weight on my chest. "I won't force you, but I need you to understand. This is serious."

The flicker of fear in Noah's eyes pushes me to a decision. "Fine. What's the plan?"

"First, we need to grab some things. I'll take you to my place where you'll be safe. We can lay low until we figure out our next steps," he explains, his voice steady and calm.

"Sounds so easy when you say it like that," I reply, forcing a laugh that feels shaky at best. "Where do you think I keep my survival gear? In the back of my closet next to the sparkly dresses?"

"Actually, that might be more useful than you think," he counters, a smirk breaking through the tension.

Ethan shoots him a look that tells him to focus. "We can't waste any time. Let's move."

We head towards the door, my heart racing. As I glance back at Ethan, I see a flicker of something—fear? Regret? It's gone too quickly for me to place it, but I want to ask. "Ethan, you're coming with us, right?"

He hesitates, his brow furrowing. "I'm not leaving you with him."

Noah bristles at the implication. "I can keep her safe, I promise."

Ethan's expression hardens. "You don't know what you're getting into. This isn't just about protection. This is about trust."

The moment feels electric, like the air before a storm, charged with unspoken words and heavy silences. "We don't have time for this," I interject, frustration bubbling beneath the surface. "I need to get out of here. You two can argue over who's better equipped to babysit me later."

Just then, the faint sound of footsteps echoes from the hallway, and my heart plummets. "Did you hear that?" I whisper urgently, my eyes darting to the door.

Noah's expression shifts, suddenly alert. "We need to move. Now!"

Ethan grabs my wrist, his grip firm. "Let's go."

As we rush towards the door, I feel the weight of the unknown crashing over me, my pulse racing. With each step, I can't shake the feeling that whatever is waiting on the other side is a chapter I'm not ready to face. As we push through the door, I hear a voice call my name from behind, smooth and chilling, cutting through the tension like a knife.

"Did you really think you could escape?"

Chapter 25: Shifting Loyalties

Ethan's words linger in the air, thick with a mixture of dread and exhilaration. I find myself tracing my fingers along the contours of the chipped wood table in my small kitchen, its surface marred by years of meals and memories, while my mind races with the possibilities that lie ahead. The shadows cast by the waning afternoon light feel heavier, almost like they're pressing down on me, urging me to make a choice. Outside, the world moves obliviously, children laughing and playing in the park across the street, their carefree joy contrasting sharply with the weight of the secrets now pressing against my chest.

"Why do you even care?" I mutter under my breath, the question aimed at nobody but myself. Why does Ethan, with his stormy eyes and secrets of his own, care about a past that seems to haunt me more with each passing day? I push back against the tight knot forming in my stomach, unwilling to acknowledge the strange mix of gratitude and annoyance I feel toward him. Perhaps it's that familiar feeling of being understood by someone who knows too well the gravity of unshakable history. Yet, the thought of being dependent on him—of letting him see the fragile corners of my heart—sends a jolt of panic through me.

I take a deep breath, my heart racing as I hear the familiar buzz of my phone. I know who it is before I look—Dylan. Somehow, he has found a way to slip back into my life, weaving himself into the fabric of my day-to-day existence like a shadow that refuses to fade. As I slide my finger across the screen, the ache of nostalgia and resentment washes over me in waves.

"Hey there, sunshine," his voice is smooth, almost teasing, sending an involuntary shiver down my spine. "I've been thinking about you."

"You've been thinking about me? How sweet," I reply, forcing a lightness I don't feel into my tone. "What do you want, Dylan?"

"Straight to the point, as always. I like that about you," he says, and I can almost see his wicked smile through the phone. "I need to talk to you about something... important. Something that involves Ethan."

My stomach drops at the mention of Ethan's name, a sinking sensation clawing at my insides. "What does Ethan have to do with anything? You know he's not part of this."

"Oh, but he is. You see, he's been looking into things he shouldn't. And I think it's time you both learned the truth," he says, his tone shifting into something more sinister, as if he knows the effect his words have on me.

"What truth?" I manage, my heart pounding as dread settles in my bones. I can feel the air thickening around me, the walls of my cozy apartment suddenly feeling like a cage.

"Meet me at the old pier tonight at eight. I promise it will be worth your while," he says before hanging up, leaving the echo of his voice lingering like a dark cloud.

The old pier has always held a strange allure, a place where laughter once echoed in the salty air, now overtaken by whispers of things left unsaid. I shake my head, trying to dispel the instinctive pull toward Dylan's request, but my curiosity wrestles with my better judgment. After all, he knows things—things about my past, about the choices that brought me to this moment.

As night falls, I dress in a simple, dark outfit, wanting to blend into the shadows. Each layer I put on feels like armor, a small protection against the inevitable confrontation ahead. The cool breeze brushes against my skin as I make my way toward the pier, my heart pounding a wild rhythm that matches the waves crashing against the wooden posts.

The moment I step onto the pier, a familiar sense of dread washes over me. The moon hangs low in the sky, its pale light spilling onto the water like spilled ink. The shadows dance, and the air is thick with tension.

"Ethan!" I call out, suddenly feeling the need for his presence. He had urged me to steer clear of Dylan, to focus on our investigation and not get tangled in the web of my past. But here I am, at the epicenter of it all, willing to confront the demons I've tried so hard to ignore.

"Looking for someone?" Dylan's voice drifts toward me, smooth and low, breaking through the silence. I turn to find him leaning casually against one of the aged wooden posts, his posture deceptively relaxed, his expression unreadable.

"Let's get this over with," I say, forcing my voice to sound steady, though my insides twist with unease.

He pushes away from the post and steps closer, the moonlight casting a sharp contrast on his features, illuminating the smirk that tugs at his lips. "You're feisty tonight. I like it."

"Enough with the games, Dylan. What do you know about Ethan?" I press, my resolve hardening. I can feel the tension stretching between us, taut and ready to snap.

"Ah, Ethan. He's quite the enigma, isn't he? But you know, he's not the only one with secrets. You've got your own, don't you?" His words are laced with a challenge, and I can feel the weight of his gaze pinning me in place, urging me to reveal my truth.

I cross my arms defensively, trying to stave off the memories that threaten to surge forward. "This isn't about me. Just tell me what you know."

Dylan chuckles, a sound that feels both dangerous and enticing. "You're more like me than you realize. But if you want the truth about Ethan, you're going to have to dig deeper—into both of your pasts. What if I told you that everything you think you know is a lie?"

The world around me seems to blur, and for a moment, the weight of his words crushes down, suffocating me in a fog of uncertainty. It's as if he's stripped away the veil that has long hidden the truth, leaving nothing but raw, pulsating fear in its place. I take a step back, needing to create space between us, the air thick with unspoken implications.

"Why should I believe you?" I challenge, though doubt begins to weave itself into my thoughts, wrapping around my reason like a serpent.

"Because, my dear," he says, his tone shifting from taunting to sincere, "you're about to find out that the lines between loyalty and betrayal are blurrier than you think. And in this game, those loyalties can shift in the blink of an eye."

The piercing realization that I'm standing at the precipice of something far more complicated than I could have ever imagined sends a chill down my spine. The world I thought I understood is crumbling, and in its place rises a tangled web of secrets, lies, and choices that could irrevocably alter the course of my life.

The sound of waves lapping against the pier becomes a hypnotic backdrop, mingling with the rapid rhythm of my heart as Dylan's words echo in my mind. My instincts scream for me to turn away, to forget about the games he plays, but curiosity pulls me in like the tide. His smirk feels both familiar and foreign, a reminder of the past I thought I had buried.

"So, what's this big truth?" I push, my voice steadier than I feel. "Are you finally going to tell me what you've been hiding, or are you just going to keep playing these little mind games?"

He chuckles, a sound that both intrigues and unnerves me. "Oh, come now. Where's the fun in that? You're smart enough to connect the dots. But first, let's consider what you really want, shall we?"

"What I want is for you to stop dragging me back into your twisted little schemes," I shoot back, crossing my arms. "But clearly, you have other ideas."

Dylan takes a step closer, the moonlight catching the glint of mischief in his eyes. "It's not just my schemes, darling. You've been a player in this game for far longer than you realize. You think you've managed to keep your secrets safe, but they're just waiting for the right moment to surface."

I step back, my heart racing. "You're wrong. I'm not like you. I didn't choose this life; it chose me."

"Ah, but isn't that the beauty of it?" he says, his tone shifting to a softer register. "We're all products of our choices, and trust me, your choices led you straight to me. And to Ethan. The question is, how deep are you willing to dive?"

The weight of his words presses heavily on my chest. It's unsettling how he knows me, yet he remains a complete stranger. "What do you want from me, Dylan?"

"I want you to see the bigger picture. To stop hiding behind the façade of normalcy. That's where the real power lies—in acceptance." His voice drips with a honeyed insincerity, laced with a challenge that's hard to ignore. "Join me, and I'll show you everything."

The thought sends a chill down my spine, but I can't help but feel a flicker of temptation. The power to reclaim my narrative has always been a siren's call, pulling me in despite the risks. But the truth? The truth could obliterate everything I hold dear, even as it offers a twisted kind of freedom.

"I'll pass," I reply, forcing an air of confidence I don't quite feel. "But nice try."

He raises an eyebrow, clearly amused by my defiance. "You're going to need to do better than that. Because soon enough, the choice won't be yours to make." He steps back, the playful glint in his eye darkening, and for a moment, I see the dangerous game unfolding behind his charming veneer.

Just as I contemplate my next move, a sharp rustling interrupts us, and my heart leaps into my throat. From the shadows emerges Ethan, his expression taut, as though he's been navigating the edges of this treacherous conversation without my knowledge. "What's going on here?" he demands, his eyes narrowing as he sizes up the tension between Dylan and me.

"Just a friendly chat," Dylan replies, the ease in his voice a stark contrast to the intensity in the air. "I was just sharing some insights with our lovely friend."

Ethan's gaze flickers to me, and in that moment, I can't read the worry or the resolve etched across his face. "You shouldn't be here, Ava," he says, stepping closer to me, his presence a comforting shield against the unpredictable chaos that is Dylan.

"Too late for that, don't you think?" I retort, trying to mask my vulnerability. "Besides, I needed answers."

Dylan feigns innocence, his grin as sharp as a knife. "Oh, she's been more than eager to unravel the mysteries of her past, haven't you, Ava? The pieces are all falling into place. You just have to trust yourself."

"Trust you?" Ethan interjects, his voice low, simmering with an intensity that sends shivers down my spine. "You can't be serious. This guy—"

"I'm serious," I cut him off, the decision hanging in the air like a charged storm. "I need to know what he knows. If we're going to figure this out, I can't keep running."

Ethan exhales sharply, frustration flashing across his features. "You don't understand what you're getting into. He's not just playing a game; he's trying to manipulate you."

"Manipulation is just another word for influence, Ethan," Dylan interjects smoothly, leaning into Ethan's space with casual arrogance. "You should know a thing or two about that, given your line of work."

"Enough!" I shout, feeling the tension radiate around us like static electricity. "I don't need you two to bicker like children. This is about me, about the choices I have to make."

Ethan runs a hand through his hair, visibly torn between wanting to protect me and needing to trust my judgment. "Ava, I can't let you get involved with him. You don't know the extent of what's at stake."

"Then tell me!" I plead, frustration bubbling to the surface. "If we're going to be partners in this mess, I deserve to know everything."

Dylan watches us with an amused glint in his eye, clearly enjoying the spectacle. "You see, Ava? The real question is who you're willing to trust. Because trust can be a double-edged sword."

Ethan takes a deep breath, his voice dropping to a whisper. "There are things I haven't told you, things about my past that connect to all of this. But you have to promise me that you'll be careful. You don't know what he's capable of."

"What are you talking about?" I demand, feeling the ground shift beneath me as layers of uncertainty unfurl. The air becomes thick with secrets, and I realize I'm standing on the brink of something monumental—something that could change everything.

Dylan's smile widens as if he can sense my growing disorientation. "Now we're getting somewhere. The real fun is just beginning, isn't it?"

"Enough of your games," Ethan snaps, taking a protective step in front of me. "This ends now."

"On the contrary, my dear Ethan," Dylan replies, his voice smooth as silk. "This is where the real game starts. But I can assure you, the stakes are higher than you ever imagined."

Before I can respond, a sudden shout pierces the night, followed by the rapid sound of footsteps approaching from behind. I spin around, adrenaline surging through me. My heart races as I realize that the looming danger is no longer just a metaphorical threat. Something is happening, and whatever it is, it's barreling toward us like a freight train, ready to upend everything I thought I understood.

The last thing I see is the glint of metal in the darkness, just before the world tilts on its axis, and everything goes black.

Chapter 26: A Dangerous Dance

I stand on the threshold of Dylan's apartment, my heart racing like a moth caught in a flame, desperate yet drawn in by the glow of his secrets. The moment he opens the door, it's as if the air shifts, charged with something electric that makes it hard to breathe. The faint smell of sandalwood and coffee lingers in the air, wrapping around me like an embrace, even as the weight of unspoken words hangs between us.

"Didn't expect to see you here," he says, his voice low, tinged with something I can't quite place—apprehension or maybe admiration. I can't tell, but it sends shivers up my spine, both thrilling and terrifying.

"Yeah, well, surprise." My words come out sharper than I intended, slicing through the tension that binds us. I step into his space, my resolve faltering slightly as the door clicks shut behind me. The apartment is dimly lit, shadows stretching across the walls, and the decor speaks of an artist's touch: splashes of color from unframed paintings lean against one another, and the air feels alive with potential, like an unfinished symphony.

He gestures toward the small kitchen nook, where a few half-empty mugs sit next to an unwashed dish. "Coffee? It's not great, but—"

"Sure, I could use a pick-me-up," I reply, though my focus isn't on caffeine but rather on the man who's pouring it. His movements are fluid, almost practiced, and I find myself captivated by the way he goes about such a mundane task, as if even boiling water is an art form in his hands.

"Would you ever tell me what's really going on?" The question slips from my lips before I can stop it, sharp and insistent. The kettle hisses, and he glances at me, the corner of his mouth quirking up into that infuriating smirk of his, one that both disarms and frustrates me.

"Do you really want to know?" he replies, his eyes glimmering with mischief, as if he holds all the cards and delights in my struggle to understand the game.

"Dylan, come on. This isn't a riddle." I lean against the counter, crossing my arms in a defensive posture that does little to hide the way my heart stutters. "You can't just drop hints like that and expect me to keep playing along."

He takes a moment, as if weighing his options, and the atmosphere thickens with anticipation. "I'm trying to protect you," he finally says, his voice steady, but I can see the flicker of uncertainty in his gaze. "There are forces at play here that you can't begin to comprehend. They've been watching you, waiting."

My stomach churns. "Watching me? For what?"

Dylan steps closer, the intensity between us palpable. "That's the thing. I don't know yet. But trust me, it's serious."

"Trust? You've got to be kidding me," I scoff, but inside, my pulse quickens. "You're the one keeping secrets."

He leans back against the counter, arms folded, the casual stance belying the tension that practically crackles in the air. "I can't just spill everything. You have to understand, this isn't just about us. There are people involved who would exploit any weakness."

"Then tell me how I'm weak," I challenge, feeling a mix of indignation and fear. "I don't want to be your damsel in distress."

The silence stretches between us, thickening with each passing moment, until he finally speaks, his voice soft but intense. "You're anything but weak. That's what makes this so complicated."

I swallow hard, caught off guard by the earnestness in his tone. "Complicated? You have no idea what complicated is," I shoot back, desperate to maintain some semblance of control in this chaotic whirlwind that is my life right now.

"Try me," he replies, a teasing spark in his eyes that sets my heart racing for entirely different reasons. "I've heard you talk about your job. All the endless hours, the judgments, the expectations. That's complicated."

His words hit closer to home than I'm prepared to admit. I glance away, grappling with the very real feeling of being seen, the rawness of my life laid bare in front of him. "It's not just about that," I whisper. "It's about feeling like I'm on a tightrope, one slip away from falling into the abyss."

"And I'm the one holding the other end," he says, a hint of gravity in his voice.

"Except you're not," I argue, the words tumbling out in a rush. "You're dancing on your own side of the line, and I'm left here trying to guess your next move."

For a moment, his expression shifts, shadows passing over his face, revealing something deeper—a vulnerability, perhaps. "I get that. But there's so much more at stake than you realize. And I can't let you wade into those waters without a life preserver."

"What if I want to dive in?" I challenge, emboldened by the simmering tension between us.

Dylan holds my gaze, the silence stretching between us as I wait for his response. Finally, he exhales, a sound that's both frustrated and amused. "You really are something else, you know that?"

"Yeah? Well, I'm glad one of us sees it."

And just like that, the conversation shifts again, like a dance that veers into unexpected territory. The wry smile returns to his lips, and I can't help but wonder if, beneath all the chaos, there's a shared rhythm we're finally learning to navigate together.

But as the night deepens, and the shadows stretch longer, the promise of truth hangs tantalizingly close yet remains just out of reach, a shimmering mirage dancing in the distance.

Dylan's gaze doesn't waver as he leans against the counter, arms crossed, the very picture of a man teetering on the edge of revealing a world I've only begun to comprehend. "I wish I could explain it all, but there are layers you need to peel back yourself." His voice is steady, but the intensity in his eyes is anything but reassuring. It sends a rush of adrenaline through me, the kind you feel just before the plunge of a roller coaster, your stomach leaping as you question your sanity for even being there.

"Peel back layers?" I echo, trying to mask my trepidation with bravado. "Am I supposed to bring a knife? Because if it's anything like my last attempt at cooking, I might just end up with a mess."

The corner of his mouth twitches, and for a brief moment, I can see the lighthearted Dylan I've grown fond of beneath the weight of the shadows that surround him. "You might need more than a knife. You'll need guts and perhaps a good therapist afterward."

"Great," I reply, rolling my eyes. "Just what I want to add to my to-do list: defuse a conspiracy and schedule weekly therapy sessions."

His laughter rings through the room, the sound brightening the dim corners and easing the tightness in my chest, if only momentarily. "You might actually be good at this. You have a knack for sarcasm that could rival my own."

I lean forward, curious yet cautious. "You think I'm joking? I'm serious. I didn't sign up for a spy thriller; I just wanted a regular life. Maybe a few plants that I won't kill and a cat named Mr. Whiskers."

Dylan's expression sobers, his teasing demeanor slipping away as quickly as it came. "Regular isn't in the cards for you anymore, not with them watching."

"Fine, let's say I believe you. What happens next? I'm not one to sit around waiting for trouble to find me."

"Then we figure out what they want," he states, his tone resolute. "I'll help you, but you need to stay close. It's the only way to keep you safe."

"Stay close? So what, I'm your shadow now?" I shoot back, feeling both flattered and irked. "Is that your way of saying I should give up my freedom? I'm not a pet, Dylan."

"Trust me, it's not that simple," he responds, his voice dropping to a murmur, a raw edge creeping in. "This is bigger than both of us. You need to understand that."

"What, like a superhero movie?" I quip, but even I can hear the tremor in my voice as the weight of his words presses against me. "I'm not cut out for saving the world. I can barely save myself."

"Then we'll save each other," he declares, and in that moment, the connection between us feels palpable, electric enough to spark a fire. But there's an undercurrent of something darker simmering just below the surface, like a hidden trap waiting for the unsuspecting to fall into its grasp.

"Okay, let's say I'm in. What's first on our heroic agenda?"

"First, we need to find out who they are and why they care about you," he replies, his eyes narrowing in thought. "There are too many unanswered questions, and we can't afford to make mistakes."

"Sounds exhilarating," I say, sarcasm lacing my words. "So, just a casual jaunt into the unknown? What could go wrong?"

He flashes a smile that doesn't quite reach his eyes. "Everything, probably. But that's the thrill of it, right?"

"Thrill? More like a heart attack waiting to happen."

As if sensing my mounting anxiety, Dylan moves closer, our proximity amplifying the tension swirling around us. "Look, I know it's a lot, but I promise you, I won't let anything happen to you."

"Famous last words," I mutter under my breath, but I can't deny the flicker of trust sparking between us, the fragile tendrils of a bond forged in uncertainty.

"Let's start with the coffee shop you work at. There's a chance someone's been lingering there, keeping tabs on you."

"Fantastic," I respond, my stomach knotting again. "I've always wanted my work to resemble a crime scene."

"Okay, so here's the plan," Dylan says, his tone shifting into something more serious, a commanding presence settling around him.

"Tomorrow, you go in as usual. I'll drop by casually. If I spot anyone, we'll figure out our next move."

"And if you don't?"

"Then we find another angle. But I won't let you go in alone."

I nod, the decision solidifying in my mind, even as a flutter of dread churns in my stomach. "All right. I guess I'm in."

"Good. We'll meet there at your usual time." He steps back, a hint of pride in his expression, and it softens the edges of the tension lingering between us. "But for now, let's just... hang out."

"Hang out? Is that code for preparing for our imminent doom?"

"Possibly," he replies, grinning. "But if we're going to do this, we might as well enjoy ourselves while we can."

The night stretches on, filled with laughter and playful banter, but even as we share these lighter moments, the underlying anxiety hums between us like an unplayed note in a symphony. I can't shake the feeling that we're on the precipice of something monumental, a tipping point that could lead to everything shattering around us.

Eventually, our conversation shifts to trivial matters—favorite movies, questionable fashion choices, and ridiculous childhood memories—yet even the laughter is tinged with a shadow of inevitability, like the calm before a storm.

As the clock ticks toward midnight, I glance at Dylan, his profile illuminated by the soft glow of the overhead lights. There's something vulnerable about him in this moment, a crack in his carefully maintained façade, and I reach out, instinctively, my fingers brushing against his arm.

"Are you scared?" I ask softly, searching his gaze.

"Every second of every day," he admits, his expression grave. "But that's why I'm fighting."

The sincerity in his voice makes my heart lurch, pulling me closer to the precipice of feelings I've tried to ignore. "And what if fighting isn't enough?"

"Then we make our own luck," he replies, determination flashing in his eyes.

Just as I'm about to respond, the shrill ring of my phone cuts through the moment, shattering the fragile bubble we've created. I fumble for my bag, a sense of foreboding settling in as I see the caller ID flash across the screen.

"Who is it?" Dylan asks, his brow furrowing.

"It's my boss."

"Answer it," he urges, tension creeping back into the room.

I hesitate, a strange unease curling in my stomach. "I don't think—"

But before I can finish, I hit "accept," bringing the phone to my ear. "Hello?"

"Where are you? You need to come in now." My boss's voice crackles with urgency, each word a sharp blade.

"Now? Why?"

"There's been a situation. We need you."

The world around me tilts on its axis, a wave of dread crashing over me as I exchange glances with Dylan, his expression darkening.

"What kind of situation?"

"Just get here. It's bad."

The call ends abruptly, leaving an echoing silence that stretches out between us, thick and suffocating. I can feel the reality of the world crashing down, the shadows closing in.

"Dylan," I say, my heart racing as panic creeps in. "Something's wrong."

And just like that, the night I thought would be about connection turns into the beginning of a new nightmare, one I never saw coming.

Chapter 27: The Edge of Oblivion

The sun hung low in the sky, painting everything in a warm, golden hue that clashed oddly with the simmering tension between Ethan and Dylan. I could almost taste the salt of the ocean mingling with the air as I stood at the edge of the pier, one foot planted firmly in Ethan's camp and the other teetering towards Dylan's world. It felt ridiculous, really, that I had become the unwilling mediator between two men who were once inseparable, a triangle formed from shattered trust and simmering resentment. The weather was perfect, but my heart felt like a storm was brewing just beneath the surface.

Ethan leaned against the weathered wooden railing, his broad shoulders tense and squared like a soldier preparing for battle. He shot Dylan a look that could curdle milk. "You think this is a game?" His voice was low and edged with the kind of anger that could spark a wildfire. I felt it in my bones, a shiver that ran from my head to my toes, as if his fury were a tangible entity hovering in the air between us.

Dylan, on the other hand, stood with an easy nonchalance, his fingers drumming against the metal of his thigh. The breeze tousled his dark hair, framing his face in a way that somehow made him look even more infuriatingly handsome. "I'm not the one playing games, Ethan. That's your specialty." His grin was disarming, but there was a coldness in his eyes that made me question everything I thought I knew about him. He looked at me, and in that moment, the world around us blurred into the background. "You know the truth, don't you?"

"Do I?" I snapped back, the words tumbling out before I could catch them. The frustration of being caught between them boiled over, bubbling up like a pot on the verge of boiling over. "You both make it sound so easy, like you're the heroes of this story, and I'm just... what? The damsel in distress?" My breath quickened, and I could feel the heat rising to my cheeks. I didn't want to be a pawn in their game, but here I was, every bit a spectator, every bit a participant.

Ethan stepped forward, his expression softening for just a moment, vulnerability flickering in his eyes like a flame barely contained. "I'm trying to protect you," he said, the anger in his voice replaced by something more fragile, more raw. "Dylan isn't who you think he is."

"And you are?" I shot back, my voice rising in pitch. "You've both been holding secrets like they're trophies, and I'm tired of being left in the dark. Maybe I don't want to be protected; maybe I want the truth." The words felt heavy as they settled between us, like stones dropped into a still pond, rippling outwards, disrupting the calm facade we'd all tried to maintain.

The air crackled with tension, and for a moment, I could almost hear the distant waves crashing against the rocks below, echoing my inner turmoil. I was an island in this tempest, surrounded by two men who felt like different halves of the same coin. One promised safety and stability, while the other whispered of adventure and unpredictability. The allure of the unknown beckoned, but so did the comfort of familiarity.

"You don't get it," Dylan said, his voice dropping to a conspiratorial whisper, a stark contrast to the harshness of our previous exchange. "There's a reason I can't walk away, and it's not just about us. It's bigger than you think." He stepped closer, his presence magnetic and disarming, as if he could pull me into his orbit with just his gaze. "You deserve to know what's really going on."

I could feel Ethan's tension radiating through the air like a charged particle, an electric current ready to spark into something explosive. "Don't listen to him!" he barked, his protective instinct flaring up once again. "He's manipulating you. Can't you see that?"

But my heart betrayed me, pounding wildly in response to Dylan's words. A part of me was drawn to him like a moth to a flame, even as another part of me fought to resist, wary of being burned. I was standing on the edge of a precipice, and the drop into oblivion felt dangerously inviting.

"Why do you keep doing this, Ethan?" I asked, voice trembling with the weight of my own confusion. "You act like you know what's best for me, but you're not the one living my life. You don't get to decide who I trust or what I want."

He opened his mouth, likely to counter with more of his usual fervor, but I cut him off, desperation clawing at my throat. "I need to hear it from him. I can't keep choosing sides without knowing the full story." The words came out as a plea, a wish for clarity in this chaotic storm.

Dylan's expression shifted, something flickering behind his dark eyes that looked almost like regret. "Okay," he said, his voice steadying as if he had finally gathered his resolve. "But if I tell you, there's no going back. You might not like what you hear."

I swallowed hard, heart racing at the prospect of the truth. Was I ready to dive into the unknown, to grasp at the threads of a story woven in shadows and half-truths? I glanced between them, the weight of their scrutiny pressing down on me like a physical force. It felt like a moment suspended in time, each second stretching into eternity as I made my decision.

"Then tell me." My voice rang clear in the dying light, the sun dipping below the horizon, leaving behind a vibrant tapestry of colors that hinted at the darkness to come. "I'm ready to know."

And in that moment, I took a step closer to the edge, daring myself to leap into the unknown.

Dylan took a deep breath, his eyes darkening with a seriousness I hadn't seen before. "Okay, here's the deal," he said, voice low but steady, as if he were about to reveal the world's greatest secret. The salty breeze tangled my hair around my face, a wild halo framing the moment like a movie scene where the stakes were impossibly high.

I shifted, feeling the rough wood of the pier beneath my feet, each plank a reminder of how precariously I was balanced on this emotional tightrope. "I'm listening," I said, and it came out steadier than I felt, as though my heart had decided to do its own thing, thumping defiantly against my ribcage.

"You know how Ethan is all about rules and structure?" Dylan began, his tone taking on that infuriatingly casual lilt that made me want to punch him and hug him simultaneously. "Well, let's just say I've been trying to shake things up. Life's not all black and white, you know?"

Ethan scoffed, crossing his arms tightly over his chest, his body language a fortress. "You call dragging people into your chaos 'shaking things up'? You've always been a reckless idiot, Dylan. It's not just about you anymore. There are consequences."

"Consequences?" Dylan shot back, his voice rising with the challenge. "What do you think this is? Some kind of dull afternoon tea? This is real life, Ethan. People get hurt, and sometimes they get saved. And sometimes, the ones who think they're saving you are actually the ones pushing you off the cliff." He turned to me, piercing blue eyes boring into mine. "I didn't want any of this to happen, especially not to you."

The weight of his gaze made my breath hitch. "What do you mean?" I leaned in, drawn closer like a moth to the flame of his confession. "What's happened? What's the real danger?"

Dylan's jaw clenched, and the muscles in his neck tensed as if he were wrestling with an internal beast. "There's something you don't know about the company Ethan works for," he said, his voice dropping to a whisper that seemed to slice through the salty air like a knife. "They've been cutting corners. There are deals going down that could destroy everything... and everyone involved."

Ethan stepped forward, frustration radiating off him like heat from a flame. "You're not helping! This isn't the time or place for your delusions, Dylan. She deserves better than your wild stories."

Dylan rolled his eyes, the flicker of amusement cutting through the tension like lightning. "I wouldn't be making wild stories if you weren't always painting me as the villain in this little drama. You're not the only one who cares about her, you know."

I felt a rush of emotion at the unexpected declaration, my heart thudding with the implications of his words. "Wait, you think I'm in danger because of work? Because of a company scandal?" My voice trembled slightly as realization dawned. "What do you know?"

Dylan looked torn, glancing from me to Ethan, and I could sense his struggle—between wanting to protect me and needing to share the truth. "I know enough to be worried, and I can't just stand by and let you—"

"Let me what?" I interrupted, feeling a strange surge of courage. "Let me wallow in ignorance? Just tell me everything." The urgency in my voice cut through the chaos, echoing in the charged air like a battle cry.

Dylan hesitated, eyes darting to Ethan, who remained unyielding, his arms crossed like a barricade. "I can't say much without putting you at risk," he replied, frustration tinged with concern. "But I've seen the files. The numbers don't add up, and there's talk of some serious misconduct—fraud, even."

A chill crept down my spine as the weight of his words settled in. "Fraud? In Ethan's company?" My mind raced, swirling with questions that threatened to overwhelm me. The implications loomed larger than the ocean waves crashing below, each one echoing the uncertainty that was settling in my gut.

"Not just fraud," Dylan continued, his voice urgent, "but people who would do anything to keep this under wraps. They're not afraid of using threats. And if they think you know something, they won't hesitate to make you disappear."

I shot a glance at Ethan, who was suddenly silent, the hard lines of his face betraying a flicker of concern. "Is this true?" I asked, my voice cracking slightly. "Is your company really involved in something like that?"

His eyes softened, and for a split second, I saw the mask he wore slip away. "It's complicated," he said, his voice low. "I didn't know about any of this until recently. But I've been trying to get to the bottom of it, to find a way to protect the people involved."

Dylan snorted. "Protecting people? Or protecting your precious job?" The bite in his tone made my chest tighten.

"Stop!" I interjected, feeling like I was in the middle of a storm that threatened to tear apart everything I held dear. "I can't do this right now. I need to think."

The waves crashed below us, a steady rhythm that somehow matched the pounding in my heart. The truth was swirling around me like the ocean mist, and I felt disoriented, caught in an undertow of confusion and betrayal.

"What if I'm in danger?" I whispered, more to myself than anyone else. The thought curled around my mind like a dark tendril, tightening its grip. "What do I do?"

Ethan stepped forward, urgency in his eyes. "We'll figure it out. You won't be alone in this. I promise."

But before I could respond, a shadow passed overhead. I glanced up, squinting against the fading light as a figure emerged from the path that led to the pier. My heart dropped as I recognized the silhouette—a tall, imposing man in a dark suit, walking with a purpose that made the hair on the back of my neck stand on end.

"Looks like someone decided to pay us a visit," Dylan muttered, his eyes narrowing as he took a step in front of me instinctively, a shield between me and the approaching figure.

Ethan moved to stand beside him, fists clenched, ready for whatever confrontation loomed ahead.

The man stopped a few feet away, his gaze locking onto mine with an unsettling intensity. "There you are," he said, a sly smile creeping across his face. "I've been looking for you."

My breath caught in my throat, and the world felt like it was tilting on its axis. The impending sense of danger crackled in the air, and I realized that this was it. The moment that would send me spiraling into the depths of the unknown, where the truth lay waiting, shrouded in darkness.

And as the realization settled in, I knew I was about to be dragged into a game that I hadn't even begun to understand.

Chapter 28: A Sudden Betrayal

The sun had dipped below the horizon, casting the park in shadows that danced like ghosts around me. I stood on the worn wooden bench, my heart a cacophony of disbelief and betrayal, the remnants of a trust that felt like shattered glass beneath my feet. Dylan had always been a paradox, an enigma wrapped in a casual smile that made my insides flutter. I had overlooked the little inconsistencies—the late-night phone calls, the furtive glances exchanged with a group I had dismissed as merely friends. I never thought they could weave a web that ensnared me so completely, that they would turn my affection into a weapon.

I replayed the moment that led to my undoing over and over in my mind, the crisp autumn air tangling around my thoughts like the leaves that rustled on the ground. I had stepped out of the coffee shop, my mind buzzing with the delight of our latest adventure—an impromptu road trip to the coast where we'd chased waves and laughter. But then, as I leaned against the sun-warmed brick wall, I heard his voice, low and conspiratorial, laced with something I couldn't place at the time. "We can't keep dragging her into this. She'll ruin everything."

Those words had sliced through the ambient noise of the bustling street like a hot knife through butter. I felt the color drain from my face as I leaned closer, hidden by a facade of shrubbery. The gravel underfoot crunched as I shifted, desperation clawing at me, urging me to make sense of this new reality.

In that moment, I could hardly breathe, not just from the shock but from the sheer weight of what I was beginning to understand. Dylan wasn't just a charming distraction; he was part of something dark and twisted, a clandestine operation that I had been blissfully unaware of. I watched him from my sheltered vantage point, his laughter mingling with the others—Greg, with his sly grin; Sarah, whose eyes sparkled with mischief; and Mark, the one I'd instinctively trusted because he had been so disarmingly earnest. How had I allowed myself to be so naïve?

Dylan leaned in closer to Sarah, their heads almost touching, and I felt the ground shift beneath my feet. It was more than a betrayal; it was a complete dismantling of the connection we had built, layer by precious layer. Suddenly, the summer nights filled with stargazing, the quiet moments spent wrapped in each other's arms, felt tainted. I had given him my heart, and he had offered me deception in return.

When I finally confronted him, it was as if I had become a character in one of those melodramatic films I used to roll my eyes at. I found him at our favorite spot—the old oak tree that had seen countless sunsets, its branches reaching out like the arms of a long-lost friend. My heart raced with fury as I stood before him, my breath coming in sharp bursts.

"Dylan, we need to talk," I said, my voice steadier than I felt.

He looked up, eyes narrowing, and for a moment, I thought I saw a flicker of guilt. But it vanished as quickly as it came, replaced by that same cold indifference that sent chills racing down my spine.

"Can't it wait? I'm kind of busy here," he replied, his tone casual, as if he were merely discussing the weather.

"No, it can't wait," I shot back, fighting to keep my voice level. "I heard you. I heard everything."

His demeanor shifted, just slightly, a muscle twitching in his jaw, but the smirk remained. "Oh, did you? You really shouldn't eavesdrop. It's a bad habit."

A knot of anger tightened in my chest, choking off the breath in my throat. "Is this how you've been treating me? As a pawn in your game?" I took a step closer, forcing him to meet my gaze. "You lied to me, Dylan. Everything you said—was it all just a strategy?"

"Not everything," he retorted, his voice dipping into something darker, more menacing. "You were fun, but you weren't part of the plan."

His words hung in the air, a chilling reminder of the emotional facade I had adored. I could almost feel the weight of the betrayal pressing down on me like the dense fog rolling in from the sea. "So what was I, then? Just a distraction while you plotted behind my back?"

"Look," he sighed, shifting his weight, his expression flickering between annoyance and amusement. "You need to understand. This is bigger than you, than us. You should have just stayed out of it."

The realization that I was merely an afterthought, a convenient thrill in his otherwise calculated existence, stung sharper than any slap. I had painted our world in vibrant colors while he had been sketching a blueprint of manipulation and deceit. My heart, once buoyant and bright, now lay in shambles, scattered like the leaves swirling around my feet.

"I trusted you," I said, my voice barely above a whisper, the betrayal settling into my bones like a winter chill. "I opened my life to you, and this is what I get in return?"

"I never asked for that," he shot back, his voice suddenly steely, an edge of anger creeping in. "You made your choices."

"I made my choices based on the person I thought you were!" I countered, the heat of my words igniting a fire inside me. "You are nothing more than a liar!"

Dylan stepped closer, the tension palpable between us, his eyes flashing with something dangerously close to resentment. "You think you know me? You don't know anything," he sneered, and for a moment, I was struck by the thought that I was staring at a stranger.

The air crackled with unresolved tension, and as the night enveloped us, I felt the weight of my shattered trust clinging to me like a second skin. I wanted to scream, to rage against the injustice of it all, but instead, I turned away, my heart heavy with loss. I would reclaim the pieces of myself he had stolen, starting now.

As I turned to leave, a weight settled in my chest, making each step feel like a punishment for trusting him. My heart, still pulsing with betrayal, thudded louder with every stride. I could hear the faint echoes of their laughter, like ghosts haunting me, mocking my foolishness. Each gust of wind tugged at my hair, as if nature itself was trying to console me, but all I felt was the chill of deception wrapping around me.

I needed air, clarity, and distance from the tangled mess that had become my life. I stumbled into the nearby café, the aroma of fresh coffee and warm pastries wrapping around me like a comforting blanket. But the moment I stepped inside, the sense of betrayal clung to me, refusing to let go. I slumped into a corner table, heart racing and mind racing faster, replaying every moment with Dylan, desperately seeking signs I had missed, clues I had overlooked.

A barista approached, her bright smile a sharp contrast to my gloom. "What can I get for you?" she chirped, oblivious to the storm brewing inside me.

"Just a black coffee, please," I replied, my voice barely rising above a whisper, betraying my own inner turmoil.

As I waited, I pulled out my phone, fingers trembling as I scrolled through the messages we'd exchanged, hoping to find a glimmer of the man I thought I knew. But instead, I found a string of sweet nothings that now felt laced with lies. I sighed heavily, resting my forehead against the cool surface of the table.

"Coffee for the heartbroken?" A voice broke through my fog, and I looked up to see a familiar face, Jenna, my friend and co-worker, standing there with an amused grin.

"More like coffee for the confused," I muttered, gesturing to the seat across from me. "Care to join? I need someone to distract me from my life choices."

She plopped down, her dark curls bouncing in rhythm with her energy. "You and me both. Work is a nightmare today. What's wrong?"

I hesitated, torn between the urge to confide in her and the fear of sounding like an emotional fool. But Jenna had a way of piercing through my defenses, her unwavering support always managing to ease the burden on my shoulders.

"Dylan," I said finally, the name tasting bitter on my tongue.

"Ah, the heartthrob with the mysterious air?" she asked, raising an eyebrow. "What has he done now?"

"Everything," I muttered. "Turns out, he's been playing me all along, keeping secrets and lying through his teeth. I overheard him talking with his friends—about me, about… everything."

Jenna's expression shifted from playful to serious in an instant. "Are you serious? What did they say?"

I recounted the painful exchange, each word a dagger, my voice laced with a mix of disbelief and anger. "I thought we were building something real, but I was just a game to him."

She shook her head, her brow furrowing in sympathy. "I'm sorry. That's beyond messed up. You deserve someone who values you, not someone who treats you like a pawn."

"Tell me about it," I sighed, my spirit deflating like a popped balloon. "I'm still processing it all, and the worst part is that I feel stupid for ever trusting him."

"Don't do that," she urged, leaning forward. "You're not stupid for wanting to believe in someone. It just means you're human."

I offered a half-hearted smile, but it quickly faded. "I just wish I had seen the signs before I fell so hard."

Jenna patted my hand, her touch a grounding force. "Let's do something fun to get your mind off him. We could hit that new escape room everyone's talking about. What do you say?"

I considered it for a moment, the thrill of the unknown tempting me. "You know what? Why not? A little adventure might be just what I need."

With a nod, she pulled out her phone, her fingers dancing over the screen as she made the arrangements. I watched her, feeling the warmth of her enthusiasm seep into my frayed emotions. But beneath that warmth lay a gnawing uncertainty, like a shadow lurking just out of sight, waiting to pounce.

A couple of hours later, we found ourselves standing in front of the brightly lit escape room venue, the neon sign flickering cheerily above us. "This place looks promising," Jenna said, bouncing on her heels, her excitement infectious.

As we stepped inside, the air shifted from the chill of the outside world to a buzzing anticipation that crackled around us. We were greeted by a host, a young man with an eager smile and a clipboard. "Welcome! Are you here for the detective challenge?"

"That's right!" Jenna said, her voice bright as we signed the waiver that felt like an ominous declaration of my life choices.

After a brief overview, we were led to a dimly lit room, decorated like an old-fashioned detective's office, complete with vintage furniture and a slightly eerie vibe. The door clicked shut behind us, sealing us in.

"Let the games begin!" Jenna exclaimed, her eyes sparkling with mischief.

We began our search, rifling through drawers filled with faux evidence and solving puzzles that led us deeper into the narrative. Laughter bubbled up between us as we worked together, the thrill of the challenge momentarily pushing aside the weight of my earlier heartache.

As we pieced together clues, I felt my phone buzz in my pocket, but I ignored it, not wanting to break the spell of distraction. Jenna was mid-sentence, her voice animated as she recounted a hilarious mishap at work, and I was grateful for the laughter echoing off the walls, chasing away the shadows lurking in the corners of my mind.

Then, just as I was about to solve the next clue, a shadow fell across the door, and my heart sank as I turned to see Dylan standing there, his expression unreadable. The room fell silent as he stepped inside, tension crackling in the air like static.

"What are you doing here?" I demanded, my heart racing, every instinct screaming at me to push him away.

"I came to talk," he said, his voice measured, but there was a desperation in his eyes that made my skin prickle.

"Talk?" I scoffed, disbelief washing over me. "You've got a funny way of expressing that."

"Please, just give me a chance to explain," he said, and I could feel Jenna's eyes darting between us, caught in the crossfire of our emotions.

I hesitated, every part of me screaming to run, to protect myself from whatever twisted game he was trying to play now. But there was a part of me, a stubborn flicker of curiosity, that wanted to hear him out. "Fine. But you better make it good," I shot back, arms crossed, heart pounding in my chest like a war drum.

Dylan took a step closer, and suddenly, the room felt too small, the air thick with unspoken words and unresolved tension. I wasn't sure if I was ready for what came next, but as his lips parted, I could sense that the game was far from over.

Chapter 29: Into the Abyss

The door creaked ominously as I stepped into the dimly lit corridor, a reluctant farewell to the familiarity of my life. The air felt thick with an electric charge, almost like the world itself was holding its breath, waiting for me to make the next move. Shadows danced along the walls, whispering secrets I was desperate to unearth but terrified to confront. My heart thrummed in my chest, a steady beat that urged me forward even as my mind screamed for retreat.

Every footstep echoed, reverberating through the silence that enveloped me like a shroud. Memories of Dylan flickered through my mind like a cruel slideshow—his laughter, the way his eyes sparkled with mischief, and the lingering warmth of his touch. Betrayal tasted bitter on my tongue, the remnants of trust now tainted by a reality I couldn't yet grasp. My fingers brushed against the wall, cold and unforgiving, grounding me as I fought the urge to run. What was I searching for, exactly? Closure? Revenge? Or perhaps an explanation that would shatter the fragile pieces of my heart into irreparable fragments?

I turned the corner, the dim light revealing an ornate door at the end of the corridor. Its surface was marked with intricate carvings, stories of ancient secrets and lost souls. My instincts screamed at me to turn back, but a strange magnetism pulled me closer, beckoning me to uncover the truth, however painful it might be. I pushed the door open with a hesitant shove, the rusty hinges groaning in protest as if they too were reluctant to share their secrets.

The room inside was a stark contrast to the darkness that enveloped the corridor. Light streamed through tall windows, bathing the space in a golden glow that felt almost surreal. Dust motes floated lazily in the beams, the remnants of forgotten dreams suspended in time. But it was the center of the room that stole my breath away. A grand table, strewn with photographs, letters, and trinkets, beckoned me to investigate. I stepped closer, my fingers itching to touch the remnants of lives intertwined, desperate to piece together the fragments of my own.

As I sifted through the items, my heart raced. There were photos of Dylan—smiling, carefree, a stark contrast to the turmoil swirling in my own heart. I found one of us, taken just weeks before his betrayal, our faces alight with laughter, eyes sparkling with promise. The world felt so innocent then, blissfully unaware of the storm brewing just beneath the surface.

"Isn't it funny how moments like these can feel like an eternity ago?" a voice drawled from the shadows, smooth and sardonic. I spun around, my heart lurching into my throat.

A figure emerged, leaning casually against the doorframe. It was Max, Dylan's older brother, with a smirk that twisted his handsome features into something almost sinister. His presence radiated confidence, but the flicker of amusement in his eyes suggested he was fully aware of the chaos his brother had unleashed in my life.

"What are you doing here?" I demanded, trying to sound braver than I felt.

"I could ask you the same thing," he replied, stepping further into the room, the light catching the edges of his tousled hair. "This is a private collection, sweetheart. Not exactly a tourist attraction."

I shot him a glare, crossing my arms defensively. "Well, your brother's the one who dragged me into this mess. I deserve to know why."

"Ah, but that's the million-dollar question, isn't it?" He leaned back, studying me with a playful glint in his eyes. "You really think he'll give you the answers you seek? Dylan has a knack for spinning tales, and he's quite the master at dodging the truth."

His words stung, igniting a spark of anger within me. "What do you know about it? You weren't the one who trusted him with everything!"

THE WEIGHT OF SILENCE

Max raised an eyebrow, a slow, mocking smile spreading across his lips. "No, but I've had my fair share of broken trust. Dylan's not the only one with secrets, you know."

I hesitated, the tension thickening the air around us. "What do you mean by that?"

His gaze flickered to the table, then back to me, and for a moment, I thought I saw a glimmer of sincerity beneath the bravado. "Let's just say there's a reason Dylan and I don't see eye to eye. And you might want to dig a little deeper before you take everything he says at face value."

My pulse quickened, curiosity intertwining with dread. I had come here seeking answers, and now I stood at the precipice of another mystery. "Why should I trust you?"

"Trust is a currency in short supply these days," he replied, his tone shifting to something almost serious. "But I can help you navigate through the chaos. If you want the truth, you're going to need allies. And right now, I'm the only one standing in your corner."

The walls seemed to close in around us as I weighed my options. I had fought too hard to unravel the knots in my life only to risk entanglement with someone who shared blood with my betrayer. But the flicker of uncertainty in Max's eyes intrigued me; perhaps he had a key to understanding what I had stumbled into.

"Fine," I said, my voice steady despite the trepidation swirling within. "But if you're playing me, I won't hesitate to cut you out. This isn't a game, Max."

His laughter echoed in the spacious room, a sound both unsettling and oddly comforting. "I wouldn't dream of it, darling. Let's see where this tangled web leads us."

As we stood there, two unlikely allies forged in the fires of betrayal, I felt the weight of my past begin to shift. The truth was waiting just beyond the horizon, and I was finally ready to chase it, no matter where it led.

A slight smile curled on Max's lips, but there was something almost feral in it, as if he enjoyed the game of cat and mouse we'd stumbled into. "So, what's the plan, my fearless detective?" he teased, leaning against the wall with an ease that belied the tension crackling between us.

I shot him a glare, crossing my arms tighter across my chest as if to shield myself from the very notion of his charm. "I'm not a detective, Max. I'm just a girl trying to figure out why the guy I trusted decided to shove a knife in my back."

"Good to know you have such high aspirations," he quipped, a grin dancing on his lips. "But let's start with the facts. You've got the betrayal, the secrets, and now you have me as your reluctant sidekick. What's the first order of business?"

I hesitated, my mind racing. It felt absurd to be standing here, plotting with someone so closely tied to Dylan. But the swirling chaos in my heart urged me to forge ahead. "I need to know what Dylan has been hiding. I need to figure out why he lied to me, and what exactly he's involved in."

"Simple enough," Max said, his tone shifting to one of mock seriousness. "Step one: find the mole. Step two: do some digging. And step three—"

"Stop," I interrupted, holding up a hand. "No more clichés. If we're going to do this, let's at least make it interesting."

He chuckled, a deep, throaty sound that sent a shiver down my spine. "You have a way of keeping me on my toes. Fine, let's make it interesting." He leaned closer, eyes narrowing as if he were truly considering how to approach the tangled web. "We need to tap into Dylan's network. There's bound to be someone who knows what he's up to."

"Who do you suggest?" I asked, my brow furrowing. "Do we start with his friends or his shady business associates?"

"Ah, but you see, that's where it gets fun." Max waved a hand dismissively. "Dylan has a knack for keeping people at arm's length. No, if you want answers, you need to go deeper. You need to get to someone who's been involved but isn't afraid of a little chaos."

My stomach tightened at the implications of his words. "You mean... a snitch? A rat?"

"Now you're catching on," he said, a smirk playing on his lips. "There's always a rat in the system, you just have to know where to look. I have someone in mind, but getting to them isn't going to be easy."

"And who exactly is this person?" I inquired, my mind racing.

He took a step back, arms crossing over his chest as he leaned against the table filled with remnants of forgotten lives. "Let's just say she has a talent for playing both sides. You'll want to tread carefully. There's a reason she's still breathing."

The way he said it sent an involuntary chill racing down my spine. "Great. How do we even approach her?"

"You let me handle that part," Max replied, confidence radiating from him. "I'll get us in. But you need to promise me something."

"What's that?"

"No heroics. This isn't your typical high school drama, sweetheart. There are real stakes here. You need to stay sharp and let me do the talking."

"Fine, I can handle that," I replied, my determination hardening like steel. "But if anything goes south, you'd better be ready to back me up."

"Trust me," he said, a playful glimmer in his eyes. "I thrive in chaos."

The thought of diving deeper into this mess with Max as my partner made my skin crawl, but I couldn't deny the thrill that coursed through my veins. Perhaps there was a chance to salvage the truth hidden beneath layers of betrayal and deception.

The two of us slipped out of the room, tension thrumming in the air between us as we made our way down the corridor. Every creak of the floorboards felt like a warning, a reminder that we were stepping into dangerous territory. I kept my gaze forward, focused on the exit, but a nagging feeling tugged at the back of my mind. What if this only led to more heartache?

"Where are we headed?" I asked, breaking the silence that hung like a thick fog.

"An old haunt of Dylan's," Max replied. "A place where he used to meet his 'friends.' It's gritty and loud, just the way you like it."

"Right," I said, sarcasm lacing my voice. "Because nothing screams 'reliable information' quite like a bar full of dubious characters."

Max chuckled, the sound a mix of amusement and admiration. "You're catching on. You know, for someone who claims to be clueless, you're doing a bang-up job of keeping up."

I rolled my eyes, refusing to let him see how much his words affected me. "Just wait until I'm actually clueless. Then we'll see how well you keep up."

As we stepped into the night, the chill of the air hit me like a bucket of ice water, the vibrant chaos of the city sprawled before us. Neon lights flashed overhead, illuminating the streets with a disorienting blend of colors. The sounds of laughter, music, and clinking glasses flooded my ears, almost drowning out the apprehension swirling inside me.

We approached a dive bar tucked away on a side street, its entrance dimly lit and crowded with people leaning against the walls, their voices a cacophony of secrets and laughter. Max led the way, his confidence cutting through the chaos like a knife. The moment we crossed the threshold, the atmosphere shifted. It felt like stepping into another world, one where the shadows held the potential for danger and excitement in equal measure.

Inside, the air was thick with smoke and the scent of cheap whiskey. My senses buzzed, and for a moment, I almost forgot about the betrayal that had driven me to this point. We weaved through the crowd, Max's posture relaxed as he navigated the sea of bodies, but I couldn't shake the feeling that we were being watched.

"Over there," Max said, nodding toward a small table in the back, shrouded in darkness. "That's her."

I squinted, trying to make out the figure seated there. A woman with fiery red hair, her demeanor exuding a mix of confidence and danger. She leaned back in her chair, eyes scanning the room with an unsettling awareness. There was something about her that both intrigued and terrified me.

"Stay close," Max murmured as we approached. "She bites."

"Fantastic," I replied under my breath, feeling a knot of anxiety tighten in my stomach.

As we reached her table, the atmosphere thickened, an electric tension crackling in the air. The woman's gaze flicked up, piercing through the haze of noise like a spotlight. Her lips curled into a knowing smile, and I realized with a jolt that she wasn't just waiting for us; she was waiting for something else entirely.

"Well, well, if it isn't the prodigal son and his charming companion," she drawled, her voice smooth and laced with amusement. "What brings you to my corner of the world?"

Max leaned against the table, an easy smile on his face, but I could feel the tension in his body, as if he were preparing for a battle. "We're looking for information, Gina. Dylan's been up to some things, and we think you might know more than you're letting on."

Her expression shifted, curiosity sparking in her eyes. "Information is a currency, darling. What do you have to offer in exchange?"

I swallowed hard, glancing at Max for support. "What do you want?"

"Oh, I think you know," she replied, her gaze piercing into mine, reading the desperation lurking just beneath the surface. "You're both in deep now, but I suspect you're not as well-informed as you think."

Before I could respond, the door slammed open behind us, the sudden noise causing a wave of silence to sweep through the bar. All heads turned as a figure strode in, confidence radiating from every step. My heart dropped as I recognized him—the familiar silhouette, the same swagger, the person I'd thought I'd left behind. Dylan.

Time seemed to freeze as his eyes locked onto mine, a silent understanding passing between us. In that instant, everything I thought I knew shattered, replaced by the realization that I was standing on the precipice of something I could never have anticipated.

Milton Keynes UK
Ingram Content Group UK Ltd.
UKHW040256181024
449757UK00001B/76